GHOST OF A CHANCE

Picking himself off the ground, Longarm saw something coming out of the darkness, something that glowed like a lantern. . . . It was the Spaniard, charging toward him, the hoofbeats of the phantom's horse thundering in the night. Longarm blinked and lifted his Colt. The Spaniard was almost on top of him.

Longarm tipped up the Colt and fired, flame geysering from the muzzle. He heard a loud *clang!* and an instant later the horse's shoulder struck him, sending him flying.

For the second time in a matter of moments, Longarm crashed to the ground. This time his head hit something hard, jolting his brain. Skyrockets went off behind his eyes. As they faded, Longarm tried desperately to avoid losing consciousness, knowing that the night was full of enemies, and if he passed out he'd likely never wake up.

The effort failed. Everything was gone, and he was lost, alone, drifting on a sea of nothingness. . . .

TABOR EVANS

LONGARM

AND THE GOLDEN GHOST

JOVE BOOKS, NEW YORK

LONGARM AND THE GOLDEN GHOST

A Jove Book / published by arrangement with
the author

PRINTING HISTORY
Jove edition / January 2004

Copyright © 2004 by Penguin Group (USA) Inc.

ISBN: 0-515-13659-X

A JOVE BOOK®
Jove Books are published by The Berkley Publishing Group, a division of Penguin Group (USA) Inc., 375 Hudson Street, New York, New York 10014. JOVE and the "J" design are trademarks belonging to Penguin Group (USA) Inc.

PRINTED IN THE UNITED STATES OF AMERICA

10 9 8 7 6 5 4 3 2 1

Chapter 1

Night over West Texas! A soft wind blew, stirring the dried pods of the mesquite trees that dotted the sage-carpeted plains. The rattle of the beans in those pods might have been the clicking and clacking of ghostly castanets played by the spirits of those who had come before, swarthy-skinned riders who dashed over the prairie on long-legged mounts, laughing and singing and daring fate. That, or the rattle of bones . . .

The huge silver-white lunar orb that floated high in the black velvet sky was the same as it had been for years, decades, centuries past, casting pallid illumination over the starkly beautiful scene. While in the millennia-long scheme of things nothing was changeless, these West Texas plains came close. On this night, they looked much as they must have looked when the Indians first came, followed centuries later by armored figures that clanked along and spoke in the soft accents of Castile.

The whole thing was enough to make a fella wax poetical if he was of a mind to, thought Longarm, as he rocked along in the saddle, riding toward the cowtown called Tascosa.

It was too bad somebody had to come along and ruin

the peaceful scene by letting off a volley of gunshots.

The spurts of Colt flame that bloomed in the darkness ahead made Longarm rein his mount to a sudden halt. The swift rataplan of hoofbeats coming toward him followed the racketing reports.

Longarm reached for his Winchester and slid the rifle from its saddle sheath. He levered a shell into the chamber and waited to see what was going to happen.

He didn't have long to wait. A yellow glow appeared up ahead, gliding through the night like a will-o'-the-wisp. The light moved at an angle, crossing in front of Longarm on a path that led northward. As the thing came closer, he got a good look at it, and what he saw made his eyes widen in disbelief.

The thing was a man on horseback, but not just any man. This one shone with an unearthly light, and instead of the rough range clothes common to the West, he wore what seemed to be armor of some sort and a metal helmet with a plume on top that trailed back in the wind of the figure's passage. If Longarm hadn't known better, he would have said that the hombre looked like one of those old Spanish conquistadors who had tramped through this part of the country a couple of centuries earlier in search of riches, in search of the fabled Seven Cities of Gold.

But that was crazy. The conquistadors were all long dead. Longarm blinked rapidly, wondering if his eyes were playing tricks on him.

Then the phantom rider, or whatever it was, swept on past him, about fifty yards away. The horses of the men chasing the glowing figure thundered closer, and once again gun muzzles geysered orange fire in a ragged volley. The bullets didn't come anywhere near Longarm. They were all directed at the fleeing rider, who by now had vanished somehow into the night.

"Hey! Over there!"

The shout came from one of the gunmen. Instantly,

2

several members of the group peeled off from the rest and charged toward Longarm. His hands tightened on the rifle. If they wanted a fight, he would give them one, but he hoped it wouldn't come to that. Maybe they'd be willing to listen to reason and wouldn't shoot first and ask questions later.

That was a futile hope, he realized a second later when he saw more flashes of gunfire. He heard the wind-rip of a slug passing close by his head.

He kicked his feet loose from the stirrups and went out of the saddle in a rolling dive. His horse let out a shrill whicker of pain and whirled around to dash off. Judging by the way the animal moved, it wasn't hurt bad. Longarm figured one of the bullets flying around had burned a hot path along the animal's flank, spooking it. The horse would probably be all right.

In the meantime, though, Longarm was set afoot, left behind as at least four riders closed in on him, men who evidently intended to kill him without bothering to find out first who he was.

They were going to be damned surprised if they shot him full of holes and then found the badge and papers that identified him as a deputy United States marshal. Those bona fides were hidden in his saddlebags, because he had decided to tackle the assignment that had brought him here incognito, at least until he'd had a chance to look around and get the lay of the land.

He might not get that chance, the way things looked now. He bellied down on the ground as more slugs sizzled around him. Bringing the Winchester to his shoulder, he fired, aiming at one of the onrushing figures that loomed toward him.

The rifle cracked sharply, followed an instant later by a scream of pain from one of the horses. Longarm bit back a curse. Given a choice, he would have preferred ventilating one of the gents shooting at him, rather than

3

a dumb animal who didn't have any say in the matter.

The wounded horse reeled and went down, falling to the side and throwing its rider. With a yell, the man sailed through the air and smashed to the ground. Then he yelled even more.

"Hold your fire! Hold your fire, damn it!"

The shouted orders rolled out in a deep, sonorous voice that drowned out the yelling of the man who had been thrown from his horse. Another rider galloped after the ones who had attacked Longarm. They reined in and stopped shooting as this man raced up to join them.

Longarm stayed where he was, another cartridge racked into the Winchester's chamber, the rifle's butt stock planted firmly against his shoulder in case the ball started up again.

The newcomer said, "What the hell are you idiots shootin' at?"

"There's a fella over here, boss," replied one of the gunmen.

"Besides the Spaniard, you mean?"

"That's right, and he shot Arch Kellman's horse out from under him!"

"That's Kellman doin' all that carryin' on?"

"I reckon."

"Well, go tend to him," said the man who seemed to be the leader of this group of gunmen. "I'll see who this stranger is."

The man paced his horse forward. Longarm trained the rifle's sights on him, but the man didn't make any threatening moves. Instead, he reined in again after a few steps and called, "Hold your fire, mister! We don't mean you any harm!"

"That's not what it looked and sounded like a minute ago!" shouted Longarm. "Those fellas with you seemed mighty intent on putting holes in my hide!"

"My boys jumped the gun," the leader said. "Can't

4

blame 'em for bein' spooked, what with that . . . *thing* . . . ridin' around. But nobody else will shoot at you, as long as you get up and tell us who you are and what you're doin' here."

Longarm was mad at being jumped for no good reason, but he was also curious about what he had seen and heard tonight. There was a good chance it all tied in with the job that had brought him here, he decided. He wanted to find out more.

So, holding the Winchester in one hand, he put the other on the ground and pushed himself to his knees, then climbed to his feet. The leader edged his horse closer.

"Well, speak up," the man prodded. His imperious tone of voice made it clear that he considered himself the big he-wolf around these parts. "Who are you?"

"Name's Parker," said Longarm, using his actual middle name as an alias, as he often did when he was working undercover. "Front handle is Custis."

"And what's your business?"

"I'm on my way to Tascosa. At least, I was until my horse ran off. Thought about making camp earlier but decided if I pushed on, I could get there before it got too late."

The man rested his hands on his saddle horn and leaned forward. "Ridin' around this part of the country at night ain't a very good idea these days. Strange things been happenin'."

"Such as being shot at for no good reason?"

"Worse than that, hombre." A hollow sound crept into the man's voice. "A whole heap worse than that." He gave a little shake of his head and went on in a more normal tone, "My boys will round up your horse. We'll even ride on into Tascosa with you. That's where we were headed when we spotted the Spaniard."

"Who?"

"Somebody you don't want to meet," the man said. "Not at night, under a Comanche moon."

The Comanches hadn't been much of a threat here in the Panhandle for the past several years, Longarm knew, not since a bunch of soldiers under the command of Colonel Ranald S. Mackenzie had wiped out their horse herd in the Battle of Palo Duro Canyon. But people who had been around West Texas for a while still referred to a bright, full moon as a Comanche moon, because the Indians had had a fondness for raiding by its light.

Longarm might have asked more about this mysterious Spaniard, but before he could, another man on foot barged up, saying angrily, "Where is he? Where's the bastard who shot my horse?"

"Take it easy, Kellman," the leader snapped.

"Easy, hell! When I fell off, I landed in a pile of prickly pear!"

Longarm managed not to laugh, realizing that such a reaction would likely make things worse. But he took some satisfaction in knowing that one of the varmints who had attacked him would be plucking cactus needles out of his hide for a while.

"That ain't this hombre's fault, now is it?" said the leader. "I'm sorry about your horse, Kellman, but right now I want you to ride double with one of the other boys. And some of you go round up Parker's cayuse, too."

The man called Kellman grumbled and cursed, but he backed off. He grasped the hand that one of the other men extended to him and swung up behind that man's saddle. He gave a little yelp as he settled down, and Longarm figured there was at least one prickly pear needle stuck in Kellman's backside.

The leader dismounted then and stepped toward Longarm, extending a hamlike hand. "I'm Charley Barfield. Got a spread southwest of here called the Box B."

Longarm shook Barfield's hand, unsurprised by the

crushing power of the rancher's grip. He returned it with strength of his own.

"You ridin' the grub line, Parker?" Barfield went on.

"That's about the size of it," said Longarm. "I figured on maybe picking up some riding work in Tascosa, since that's the supply point for all the ranches around here."

"Ever been in these parts before?"

"Nope," Longarm lied. His work had taken him to just about every corner of the West, often more than once. Even before he had started packing a badge for Uncle Sam, a brief spell of honest-to-gosh cowboying had brought him to the Texas Panhandle, back when Goodnight and Loving and the other pioneer cattlemen had been just getting a foothold here. That had been in the days not long after the end of the Late Unpleasantness, before hoof and horn had brought Texas back from the brink of economic ruin. The cowboys, of whom Longarm had been one, had had a lot to do with saving the Lone Star State.

That was in the past now. The great cattle drives were over. But the vast, sprawling ranches remained and flourished, with their herds being driven only as far as the stockyards at Fort Worth, which had been reached a few years earlier by the shining rails of the Texas & Pacific Railroad.

So it was certainly possible, thought Longarm, that he could run into someone who might recognize him, but he had to take the chance. It was just as likely that he wouldn't encounter anyone who knew him as a lawman.

"Well, if you're a decent hand, you'll likely find work," said Barfield. "With those Eastern syndicates comin' in, and even folks from England buyin' ranches, there are cattle spreads all over these parts. In the meantime, I'll stand you to a drink at the Deuces Saloon, to sort of pay you back for my men jumpin' you like that. It's the best waterin' hole in Tascosa."

"Much obliged," said Longarm. "I'll take you up on that."

He was at least as interested in information as he was in a drink. Maybe Charley Barfield could tell him more about the wave of lawlessness that had swept over the Panhandle in recent months, the reign of terror that had brought Longarm to Texas in the first place.

Chapter 2

"It's stretching things a mite to call this a federal case," Chief Marshal Billy Vail had told Longarm a week earlier in Vail's office in Denver. "Rustling, murder, robbery, things like that are all state crimes. But several of those big ranchers down there in the Panhandle have beef contracts with the Army, and if something is interfering with their ability to make delivery on those contracts, I see that as justification enough for action by our office."

Longarm cocked his right ankle on his left knee as he sat in the red leather chair in front of Vail's paper-littered desk. He snapped a lucifer into life on his thumbnail and held the flame to the tip of the cheroot clamped between his teeth. When he had the cheroot going, he shook out the match and dropped it on the floor beside the chair. Taking a deep drag, he blew out the smoke in a near-perfect ring and said, "Plus one of your old pards from the Rangers asked you for a hand, didn't he, Billy?"

"McDowell's got a man he usually sends out on jobs like this," Vail admitted, "but the fella's laid up right now with a bullet through his lungs and a broken leg from his last assignment. So the captain sent me a wire asking me if I had a good man I could spare." Vail paused and then

9

added caustically, "Since I don't, we'll just have to make do with you, Custis."

Longarm grinned and said, "It's a good thing I know you're joshing, Billy, else I might up and take offense."

Vail ran a hand over his pink scalp and then shoved a sheaf of papers across the desk toward Longarm. "Take a look at those reports."

For the next few minutes, Longarm smoked the cheroot and read through the documents he took from Vail's desk. They were copies of reports filed by county sheriffs and town marshals from all over the Texas Panhandle. The reports told of banks looted, stagecoaches held up, cattle herds run off by night . . . and killing after killing.

Longarm glanced up. "That Ranger captain thinks one bunch is responsible for all this hell-raising?"

"There are enough similarities between the crimes to make it possible. There could be more than one gang of owlhoots operating down there, of course. You know how outlaws are. If they hear a place is lacking in law, they flock to it like vultures on horseback."

Longarm nodded slowly. "Considering how close most of those ranches are to the New Mexico border, the wide-loopers wouldn't have any trouble running stolen stock over the line and selling it to cattle buyers over there. Most of those fellas ain't too particular about brands or bills of sale or things like that." He put the cheroot back in his mouth and chewed on it for a moment. "Some of these killings don't seem to tie in, though. There's no good reason for them that I can see."

"Well, that's one more answer you'll have to root out," said Vail. "*If* you take the job."

Longarm arched an eyebrow. "You giving me a choice, Billy?"

"Under the circumstances, I'd rather not order you to accept this assignment, Custis. Like I said, we're stretching a point to say that it falls under federal jurisdiction."

10

Longarm thought about it. He knew Vail had ridden for the Texas Rangers for years before he had gone to work for the Justice Department as the chief marshal for the Western District. Vail's ties to the Rangers were still strong. And those Texans were proud, as Longarm well knew. If that captain down in Austin had wired Billy Vail for help, then the situation in the Panhandle had to be mighty bad. Just the sort of thing it would be a real challenge to clean up . . .

A grin spread across Longarm's face, under the sweeping mustaches. "Sure, Billy, I'll take the job," he said. "Sounds like fun."

Vail snorted. "Only a wild man like you would think so." His tone softened. "But I appreciate it, Custis. I really do."

Longarm waved away the gratitude. "Don't start in on the hearts and flowers. I just want to get out of Denver for a while. I been around here so much lately Henry ain't even snarling at me no more. I think he's getting used to me, God forbid."

Henry was the spectacle-wearing young fella who played the typewriter in Vail's outer office and handled all the paperwork for the chief marshal. He and Longarm had been adversaries for a long time, and Longarm didn't want anything interfering with that. He suspected that Henry didn't, either.

"How do you figure to start?" Vail asked as Longarm got to his feet.

"Same as always," said Longarm. "I'll stir things up a mite and see if I can't get somebody to shoot at me."

Well, he had accomplished that, all right, he thought now. And he had managed not to get ventilated in the process, which was always a good thing.

Several of Barfield's cowboys had caught Longarm's horse. They led it back and one of them handed him the

11

reins. The one called Kellman said, "I ought to get that horse, since he shot mine."

"Shut up, Arch," Barfield said. "I told you, that was your own fault."

Longarm checked over his mount by moonlight and found the bloody scrape on its hindquarters where a bullet had burned it. A little ointment at a livery stable in Tascosa would take care of that. He swung up into the saddle and pulled the horse over beside Barfield's mount.

"Reckon I'm ready to ride."

"Let's go, then." Barfield hipped around in his saddle and raised his voice to speak to his men. "Keep an eye out. No tellin' what we'll run into."

The group rode east. "We were on our way to town when we spotted the Spaniard," Barfield said to Longarm. "We lit out after him; otherwise we wouldn't have been off the trail like this. Did you see him?"

"Fella on horseback, shining like gold and wearing armor?" Longarm felt faintly ridiculous just saying it.

"That's him, all right," Barfield responded grimly. "Now that I think about it, chasin' after him like that was a damned foolish thing to do. Even if you could catch a ghost, what do you do with it once you've caught it?"

"Ghost?" repeated Longarm.

"That's right. Some folks say it's the ghost of old Coronado himself. They say his spirit is cursed to wander these plains until he finally finds Cibola and Quivira and all them other lost cities of gold he was lookin' for so long ago."

"He's going to have a hard time doing that," said Longarm, "since more than likely those places don't exist and never did. Assuming, of course, that the fella we saw is really Coronado's ghost."

Barfield shook his head. "I've never believed that. The Spaniard ain't Coronado's ghost, that's for sure."

"Glad to hear you think so."

"Yeah, Coronado's armor was a lot fancier than what the Spaniard wears," continued Barfield. "That fella's the ghost of a regular conquistador, one of Coronado's soldiers."

Barfield's tone was utterly serious as he spoke, and when Longarm glanced over at him he saw that the rancher's face was solemn in the moonlight. Barfield believed what he was saying.

Longarm remained silent for a moment, letting the time stretch out. Finally, he said in a deliberately dubious tone, "I don't know if I want to work around here or not, if you've got ghosts in glowing armor galloping around."

"That's not all the Spaniard does. Some folks call him the Bloody Spaniard, because wherever he shows up, somebody dies not long after, usually in a mighty bad way."

"Well, then, since you boys were chasing him tonight—"

"Don't say it," Barfield broke in with a shudder. "I've already thought about it. That's one reason I wish we hadn't been so quick to go after him." His voice grew hollow. "I figure the curse is on us now. If all of us live through the night, I'll be damned surprised."

Longarm looked askance at the cattleman. "Maybe I shouldn't be riding with you."

"Probably not, if you value your hide."

Longarm was hardheaded enough not to believe in ghosts or any other sort of haunt. But he had seen a few strange things in his life, things he couldn't really explain. He indulged his curiosity and said, "Tell me more about that."

"I reckon you got a right to hear it, seein' as how you're not from around here and didn't know what you were gettin' into." Barfield rubbed a hand over his jaw, the callused palm rasping against beard stubble. "The Spaniard showed up about three months ago, on the same night

13

somebody rustled old Jephtha Cummings's herd and killed Jephtha and three of his ranch hands. Only one of the men who rode for Jephtha lived through that night, and he claimed he saw the ghost of a conquistador riding along the ridge above the bed-ground where the cattle were being held, just before the rustlers hit the herd, all guns a-blazin'. A week later, the bank over at Mobeetie was robbed in the middle of the night. Owlhoots used dynamite to blow the vault door right off its hinges, then shot their way out of town when folks tried to stop them. Two men were killed there, gunned down without mercy. And a couple of witnesses say they saw the Spaniard riding down the street just before all hell broke loose."

"So somebody's dressing up in armor and leading a gang of outlaws," said Longarm. "Wouldn't be the first time such a thing has happened." As a matter of fact, he himself had dealt with armor-wearing bandits in the past.

"Odd as that sounds, I reckon you could be right," admitted Barfield. "But nobody ever sees the Spaniard take part in the crimes. He's just there before they start, then gone. Same thing happened in a couple of stage holdups, another bank robbery, and on four separate occasions when stock has been rustled. That ain't the worst of it, though."

Longarm remained silent this time, knowing that the garrulous cattleman would tell him what else the mysterious Spaniard had been involved in.

"Half a dozen times," said Barfield, "folks have seen the Spaniard lurkin' around Tascosa. He always slips away before anybody can grab him, just like he did tonight. And each time he's been seen like that, a body has been discovered not long after, always close by. Sometimes they're shot, sometimes they've been stabbed, and once . . ." A shudder ran through Barfield's burly frame. "The fella looked like he'd been beaten to death with a blacksnake or some other sort of whip."

14

Longarm frowned. "And these killings take place by themselves, without a robbery or any other sort of crime going on at the same time?"

That question was the sort that a lawman would ask, but if Barfield noticed that, he gave no sign of it. Instead he said, "That's right. Just the murders. Nobody knows what the dead men did to get the Spaniard mad at them."

"Who were they?"

"One was a newspaperman, Pete Brandywine by name. He'd just started up a paper in Tascosa. Nobody took it over after he died. Then there was Fletch McAuliffe, one of the sheriff's deputies. And Hobart Rhone, who owned a general store in town." Barfield shrugged. "The other three were strangers. Drifters, from the looks of them, cowboys ridin' the grub line like you, Parker. Nobody really knew them."

"Sounds like I've got a reason to worry, right enough," mused Longarm. "This Spaniard seems like a real hell-bender."

"Nobody who stops to think about it dares cross him." Barfield jerked a thumb over his shoulder at the men riding behind them. "Of course, stoppin' to think lets this bunch out entirely. Sad to say, I got carried away and went along with 'em when they lit out after the ghost tonight."

"I was a mite busy at the time, what with being shot at and all," Longarm said dryly, "but I didn't see what happened to the fella you were chasing. Where did he go?"

"Damned if I know. He was there one minute, then gone the next. But I reckon if you're a ghost, you can do things like that."

"I reckon," said Longarm, but he was thinking that the Spaniard had to have gone *somewhere*. If he got a chance, it might be a good idea to ride out here again in daylight and take a look around.

A few minutes later, lights came into view up ahead,

twinkling like fireflies in the darkness. "That's Tascosa," Barfield said, nodding toward the lights. "Wildest town on the Staked Plains."

"As long as I can get a drink and something to eat, and find a place to lay my head, it's all right with me," said Longarm truthfully. He was thirsty, hungry, and tired after the long trip from Denver, accomplished by train, stagecoach, and now on horseback.

Barfield said, "You can get all those things at the Deuces. Like I told you, it's the best saloon in Tascosa, and they put on a decent feed, too. Rooms upstairs for rent."

"Does a painted lady go with the room?"

"Not in the Deuces," replied Barfield with a shake of his head. "Lady Arabella don't allow that sort of carryin' on."

Longarm looked over at him. "Lady Arabella?"

"The gal who owns the place. Lady Arabella Winthrop. An Englishwoman, and as pretty as they come."

That got Longarm's interest equally as much as the prospect of a drink, a hot meal, and a place to sleep. He'd been accused of having an eye for a pretty girl, and he had never bothered denying the accusation.

The lights grew bigger and closer as the group rode on into the settlement. Besides the Deuces, Tascosa had numerous other saloons, and all of them seemed to be doing a brisk business. Horses were lined up at the hitchrails in front of the saloons, and men moved back and forth on the boardwalks that lined both sides of the dusty street. Other establishments besides the saloons were still open as well. Longarm saw a couple of general mercantiles that were lit up, with customers coming and going, and a dance hall, a shooting gallery, a barbershop, and a blacksmith also showed lights. The cowboys from the surrounding ranches couldn't always make it into town during the day, so the local merchants had to take their trade whenever they could.

The Deuces was in a large building that took up an entire block on one side of the street. The sign on the awning that overhung the boardwalk in front of it was decorated with paintings of playing cards, all of them twos except for a scattering of jacks, queens, kings, and aces. There was a batwinged entrance at each corner. Bright light spilled through the long glass windows between the two doors.

The group from the Box B reined in and dismounted, Longarm among them. Finding room for the horses at the mostly full hitchrack was difficult, but the men managed. As Longarm tied the reins of his mount around the wooden pole, he felt eyes on him and glanced over to see the cowboy named Arch Kellman glaring at him. The flat planes of Kellman's face were still dark with anger over the killing of his horse.

Longarm knew he had made an enemy in Kellman. He told himself it would be wise to keep an eye on the man.

At the moment, though, he had more pressing interests. Barfield clapped a hand on his shoulder and said, "Come on, let's go get that drink."

The men had started toward the steps that led up to the boardwalk when a yell suddenly rang out. Hoofbeats rumbled close by. Longarm swung around to see that a wagon drawn by four horses had come careening around a corner. The horses were wild-eyed, snorting, out of control.

And they stampeded straight toward the group of cowboys from the Box B.

Chapter 3

With startled, frightened shouts, the men tried to throw themselves out of the path of the runaway team and wagon. Longarm was close to the boardwalk, so with a bound he leaped onto the planks and turned back to grab Charley Barfield's vest. He yanked the burly cattleman out of harm's way.

The other men all jumped and scurried to safety, with one exception. A gangling, long-legged cowboy with a thatch of bright red hair under a battered Stetson got his booted feet tangled together as he turned to run. With a scream, he fell.

There was no time, and nothing anyone could do to save him. Longarm grimaced and looked away as the thunder of hoofbeats and the creaking of wagon wheels cut short the terrified scream.

"Rance!" Barfield bellowed.

The runaway wagon swept past and continued rolling down the street, leaving behind a bloody shape huddled in the dirt. Four sets of hooves had pounded the luckless cowboy into the ground, pulping flesh and bone. Iron-rimmed wheels had finished the grisly job. The cowboy had never had a chance.

His friends gathered around him, horrified expressions on their faces. Barfield bulled his way through the ring of men and went to one knee beside the smashed shape. He checked for a pulse and then, with a mournful shake of his head, straightened to his feet.

"Dead," Barfield declared, though no one with eyes really needed that assessment confirmed. "The poor son of a bitch."

The commotion had drawn plenty of attention. Men poured out of the Deuces onto the boardwalk to see what was going on. They parted abruptly to let a slender figure through, and as Longarm glanced in that direction, he got his first look at the woman who had to be Lady Arabella Winthrop.

She was every bit as lovely as Barfield had said. Tall and slim, she wore a high-necked gown that did little to conceal the curves of her body. Her midnight black hair was piled high on her head in an elaborate arrangement of curls. She wasn't a classic beauty. Her mouth was a little too wide, her jawline a bit too defiant for that. But Longarm was immediately drawn to her anyway, and when she turned away from the gruesome sight in the street and her eyes met his for a moment, he saw an answering flash of interest.

"What happened, Charley?" she asked Barfield. Her quiet, well-modulated voice held only a trace of a British accent. Longarm had no idea what an English gentlewoman was doing here in a wild Texas cowtown, but evidently she had been away from her native shores for a while, long enough to lose some of her accent, anyway.

"I don't rightly know," Barfield told her. "A runaway wagon came out of nowhere and ran over Rance. The team trampled him, and then the wagon rolled over him, too. The rest of us managed to get out of the way, but Rance was unlucky enough to slip and fall. I reckon I know why he was unlucky, too." Barfield paused for a second. When he went on, Longarm knew what he was going to say. "It was the curse of the Bloody Spaniard."

"What?" Lady Arabella exclaimed in surprise. The men who had come from the Deuces looked at Barfield in amazement.

The cattleman dragged the back of a hand across his mouth. "We saw him on the way into town tonight. The ghost, I mean. He had that armor on, just like everybody says, and he was shinin' like gold. One of the boys let off a shot at him without thinkin'—" Barfield stopped short, and his eyes widened as he remembered what had happened. "It was Rance," he said hollowly. "Rance was the one who took the first shot at the ghost and started chasin' after him. And now he's *dead*!"

Shocked murmurs came from the crowd gathered on the boardwalk and in the street. As for Longarm, he wasn't surprised by Barfield's revelation. But that didn't mean he lent any credence to what Barfield obviously was thinking. The tragic accident that had befallen the young cowboy called Rance didn't have to have any connection with the events of earlier in the evening.

But Longarm had to admit it was sort of strange. For one thing, there had been no driver on the seat of that wagon, and yet the team had turned the corner and come straight at the Box B cowboys, including Rance. And now the wagon was gone. Longarm looked up and down the street but didn't see the vehicle and its team anywhere.

They had vanished just like that glowing figure on horseback . . .

Longarm gave a little shake of his head. If he let his imagination run away with him, he would be that much farther away from solving the mysteries that had brought him to the Texas Panhandle. He had to stick to facts. Cold, hard facts.

A beefy, middle-aged man with a slight limp came along the street, the light from the windows shining on the star pinned to his vest. When he saw Rance's disfigured corpse, he exclaimed in a high-pitched voice, "Lordy mercy, what happened here?"

"An accident, Sheriff Thurston," said Lady Arabella. "This poor man was killed by a runaway wagon."

"Plumb trampled to pieces, as well as run over," said the sheriff. "Well, I'll have Barney Oglesby come down and take him back to the undertakin' parlor."

The lawman seemed satisfied with that decision and evidently didn't intend to ask any more questions. Longarm frowned. If he had been in charge of the investigation into the cowboy's death, he would have wanted more details.

He wasn't in charge, he reminded himself. He was pretending to be just an average cowhand himself, sporting well-worn range clothes instead of the brown tweed suit he often wore while on official business.

Thurston might be satisfied with Lady Arabella's explanation, but Charley Barfield wasn't willing to leave it like that. He said, "It was the Spaniard who did it. We saw his ghost out on the prairie, and Rance shot at him. Hell, we all shot at him."

The sheriff looked pained. "Aw, why'd you want to go and do a thing like that for?" he asked in a plaintive voice.

"We lost our heads. It was a damned stupid thing to do."

"I'll say it was. Well, you see what comes o' crossin' the Bloody Spaniard," said Thurston.

The matter-of-fact way in which he spoke told Longarm that the sheriff fully accepted Barfield's story and agreed that the ghost was to blame for Rance's death. Several men in the crowd nodded knowingly in response to Thurston's comment. Longarm wondered if the whole town had gone soft in the head. They were mighty quick to blame a ghost for what had happened.

The sheriff limped off to fetch the undertaker as the

crowd dispersed. Most of them went back into the Deuces. Longarm, Barfield, and the other men from the Box B joined them.

The empty space at the bar filled up quickly. Longarm found himself standing next to Barfield. He hooked a boot heel on the brass rail as Barfield motioned to Lady Arabella, who had gone behind the long, gleaming length of polished hardwood. She made her way down the bar to join them.

"Who might this be, Charley?" she asked Barfield as she looked at Longarm. "A new hand?"

"No, but he's lookin' for work. I haven't hired him myself because my crew's full right now. Lady Arabella, meet Custis Parker."

She extended a cool, slim hand and smiled as Longarm took it. "Mr. Parker," she said. "I'm pleased to meet you."

"The pleasure is all mine, ma'am," said Longarm.

"Where are you from, if you don't mind my asking."

"Nope. I hail from West-by-God Virginia. It's been a long time since I was there, though. Left right after the war."

"Did you take part in that unfortunate conflict?"

"Yes, ma'am, but don't ask me which side I was on." Longarm grinned. "It's been so long, I sort of disremember."

"My father was in the Foreign Service," she said. "For a time there was talk of Britain entering the war on the side of the Confederacy. That could have made quite a difference in the outcome, I expect."

Longarm shrugged. "Wherever a fella goes, there's always roads not taken. Best not to worry over-much about what's down 'em, I always say."

"That strikes me as a wise bit of philosophy, Mr. Parker."

"Call me Custis," he said.

"Very well. Would you like a drink, Custis?"

Barfield said, "He sure would. And I'm payin' for it." He dropped a coin on the bar. Even over the hubbub in the room, the ringing sound it made was clearly audible. "I could use a snort, too."

Lady Arabella didn't pour the drinks herself. Instead she motioned to one of several bartenders who were working behind the hardwood. He took a bottle from under the bar and splashed whiskey into clean glasses. Longarm would have preferred some Maryland rye, but when he sipped the liquor he found it smooth and fiery at the same time. He nodded in approval.

"By the way, Charley," said Lady Arabella, "not to point out the obvious and the unpleasant, but after what happened to poor Rance, you don't have a full crew on the Box B anymore."

Barfield's eyes widened in realization. "By Godfrey, you're right, ma'am. I don't." He turned to Longarm. "If you're still in the market for a job, I can use a good man, Parker."

Longarm had made it clear that he was looking for work, so he couldn't turn down Barfield's offer without seeming suspicious. A grub line rider such as he was pretending to be usually wasn't too picky about employment.

"Sure," he said with a nod. "I'm obliged, Mr. Barfield. Or I reckon I should say, boss."

"Call me Charley," declared Barfield. "I ain't one to stand on ceremony."

"All right, Charley. Thanks."

Barfield turned back to Lady Arabella. "Custis needs a hot meal, too. You reckon that cook o' yours could rustle him up a steak and all the trimmin's?"

She smiled. "I think we can manage that. Are you paying for this, too, Charley?"

"Yeah." He added to Longarm, "But you can count the meal as an advance against your wages. I don't mind buyin' a fella a drink, but I ain't made o' money, you know."

"That's fine," agreed Longarm. "I'll owe you."

"Since you're a newcomer to our fair town, the house will also buy you a drink," Lady Arabella offered. "Why don't you take it over to that table while it's vacant? That situation may not last for long."

Longarm nodded and picked up his glass after the bartender refilled it. He and Barfield walked over to the empty table and sat down.

As Longarm sipped the whiskey, he had a chance to look around and study the patrons of the Deuces. They were a typical bunch, a mixture of cowhands, townsmen, gamblers, and a few women in bright, spangled dresses. Barfield had said that no whoring went on upstairs in the saloon, but judging by the amount of attention the women received and the whispered conversations they had with some of the men, Longarm figured business arrangements were being made for later in the evening at some other location. Evidently, Lady Arabella didn't care if her girls charged for it; she just didn't want the deals consummated under her roof.

Sheriff Thurston came in a short time later, accompanied by a man in a dark tan suit and a broad-brimmed white hat with a peaked crown. The man had a leathery look about him, as if he had spent most of his life in the sun. He wore rimless spectacles and had iron gray hair under his hat. He didn't seem to be a cattleman, but he wasn't a townie, either, Longarm judged.

"Who's that?" he asked quietly, leaning toward Barfield as he spoke.

"You mean the gent with Sheriff Thurston? His name's Chapman. Some sort of professor from back east. He's been out here for a few months, pokin' around."

"Poking around for what?"

"Artifacts, he calls 'em." Barfield frowned. "Come to

think of it, that's a mite odd. Chapman's studyin' ol' Coronado and tryin' to figure out the exact route he took when he was searchin' for the Seven Cities of Gold. I hear tell he's come across several things that the soldiers dropped or left behind for some reason, like old Spanish bits and things like that."

Longarm nodded slowly. He ran a thumbnail along his jawline and then tugged briefly at the lobe of his right ear, habits he had when he was deep in thought. He had crossed paths with archaeologists, geologists, and other sorts of scientists and professors several times in his eventful career.

And such encounters hardly ever turned out peacefully. For some reason, those scientist fellas always seemed to attract trouble. Longarm hoped that wouldn't be the case here.

Thurston and Chapman went to the bar for a drink. They were still there a few minutes later when one of the bartenders brought a platter of food over to the table where Longarm and Barfield sat. The steak was fried up just right, Longarm discovered as he cut it and took a bite, and the mountain of fried potatoes with it were equally tasty.

Lady Arabella came over to sit down with them. "Save some room for deep-dish apple pie," she advised Longarm. "I have a Chinese cook who makes the best pie this side of San Francisco."

"I'll keep that in mind, ma'am." Longarm chewed happily.

As he ate, he found himself growing drowsy. He said to Barfield, "Charley, would you mind if I didn't ride out to the Box B until tomorrow? I sort of had my heart set on a night's sleep in a nice soft feather bed, and I don't reckon your bunkhouse is furnished with such-like."

Barfield snorted. "I hope to smile it ain't. The bunks ain't too bad, but they can't hold a candle to what Lady

Arabella offers upstairs. I suppose you want another advance on your wages to pay for a room?"

"No, this fine meal is enough. I think I can scrape up the cost of a room for one night."

"In that case, we'll see you tomorrow." Barfield got to his feet. "I'll round up the boys. We got a long ride back home."

"Watch out for the Spaniard on the way," Lady Arabella cautioned.

Barfield's face was grim as he replied, "You can bet a hat on that. And if we see him, this time we're goin' the other direction."

He gathered his punchers, and the group trooped out of the saloon. Arch Kellman had been drinking steadily at the bar, and he shot Longarm a dark look before he slapped the batwings aside and stepped out into the night. Lady Arabella noticed the cowboy's attitude and commented to Longarm, "Kellman doesn't seem to like you very much."

"I sort of shot his horse out from under him earlier tonight."

Elegantly plucked and curved eyebrows arched. "Really?"

As he was finishing up his pie, Longarm explained how he came to be riding with Barfield and the other men from the Box B. "I reckon it's safe to say Kellman's got a grudge against me now," he concluded.

"You had better be careful," said Lady Arabella. "He's a dangerous man. Most of Charley's riders are just the usual sort of cowhands, but Kellman has a bit of a reputation as a gunman. I daresay that's why Charley hired him."

"Come again?" said Longarm.

"Kellman went to work for the Box B only a few months ago, right after the rustling started. I suppose

Charley felt that he needed a tough man on his side if the rustlers came after the Box B."

"Have they?"

Lady Arabella shook her head. "Not so far, at least not that I'm aware of. Charley's been quite fortunate."

"Uh-huh," said Longarm, ostensibly agreeing. Actually, he wondered if luck really had anything to do with the fact that the rustlers hadn't hit Barfield's spread.

"Well, I suppose you'd like to turn in. I'll show you to your room."

That offer from Lady Arabella caught Longarm's attention. He didn't figure she meant anything suggestive by it, but you never could tell . . .

"That sounds fine, ma'am. Lead the way."

Chapter 4

As it turned out, she *didn't* mean anything suggestive by it. She just took him upstairs, showed him to his room, and left him there with a smile and a polite "Good night."

Longarm went back downstairs and got his horse from the hitchrack, leading it down the street to the nearest livery stable. Once he had arranged with the hostler to care for the animal and store his saddle, Longarm took his Winchester and saddlebags and returned to the Deuces. He had noticed a set of rear stairs that led to the second floor, so he used them rather than going back through the crowded barroom.

The door at the top of the stairs was unlocked. He opened it and stepped into a corridor that ran the width of the building at the back. Another hallway intersected it halfway to the other end. Longarm knew his room was off that hall, which led to the balcony overlooking the saloon's main room downstairs.

The corridor had a carpet runner, so his boots didn't make much noise as he entered. The man who stood at the corner of the other hall with his back to Longarm didn't seem to have noticed him. The man had a gun in his hand, held close to his ear, with the barrel pointing toward the ceiling. As Longarm watched, the man slipped furtively around the corner and into the other hallway.

Now there was a fella who was just bound to be up to no good, thought Longarm.

Carefully, silently, he set his saddlebags and rifle on the floor and catfooted toward the corner. His hand went to the butt of the Colt .45 in its cross-draw rig and smoothly palmed out the revolver. He stopped just before he reached the corner and took off his flat-crowned, snuff brown Stetson. Leaning forward, he edged an eye past the corner to take a look.

The gunman had paused in front of one of the doors. Longarm wasn't surprised to see that it was the door to the room Lady Arabella had given him.

As Longarm watched, the gunman lifted a foot, drawing it back in preparation for a kick that would bust the latch and slam the door open. Once the man was inside, Longarm figured he would empty that pistol into the bed, thinking to catch his quarry there asleep.

Instead, before the would-be killer could launch his attack, Longarm stepped around the corner and said quietly, "I wouldn't do that if I were you, old son."

Startled and caught by the unexpected challenge off-balance with his foot up, the gunman reeled backward and ran into the other wall of the corridor. As he bounced off the wall, he twisted and tried to bring his gun around to bear on Longarm.

But Longarm's Colt was already drawn and leveled. He warned sharply, "Drop it!" He wanted to take this hombre alive, so that he could question him and find out who had put him up to this job of murder. All it had taken was one glimpse of the man's beard-stubbled face for Longarm to know that he'd never seen him before.

Instead of heeding the warning, the gunman snarled a curse and fired. The shot was rushed, but even though it missed, the slug came close enough to Longarm's head

30

for him to hear the wind-rip of its passage. He had no choice but to return fire.

He aimed low, figuring to shoot a leg out from under the gunman. As the Colt roared and bucked in Longarm's hand, however, fate intervened. Still off-balance, the man fell, going to a knee. That brought him to just the right level so that Longarm's bullet tore through his abdomen.

Gut-shot, the man toppled over onto his face with a groan. He dropped his gun. It skidded away over the carpet runner. Longarm bounded forward and kicked the fallen revolver even farther out of the gunman's reach. He knelt beside the wounded man, grasped his shoulder, and rolled him onto his back.

The man stared up at Longarm through eyes that were wide and bulging with pain and disbelief. "You . . . you shot me!" he gasped.

Longarm didn't waste time pointing out that the man had tried to do the same thing to him. Instead he said, "Who sent you here? Who wanted me dead?"

The gunman's eyes started to glaze over. A wound such as the one he had suffered, while almost always fatal, seldom killed its victim right away. Gut-shot men often took hours to die. But they could lose consciousness and spend those remaining hours out cold, beyond the reach of any questioners. Longarm didn't want that to happen here. He shook the wounded man's shoulder, trying to prod him into hanging on to consciousness.

It didn't work. The man rasped, "Gold . . . golden . . . armor . . ." and then his eyes rolled up in their sockets. A breath rattled in his throat.

Surprised, Longarm looked down at the man's lower body. It lay in a large pool of blood. His bullet must have nicked an artery, he thought, and the gunman had bled to death in a matter of moments. Grim-faced, Longarm checked for a pulse in the man's neck. When he didn't find one, he knew he was right. He had misjudged the severity of the wound.

Not that it would have mattered if he hadn't. Even if he had known that the gunman was on the verge of death, he would have asked the same question.

The answer he had gotten was intriguing, too. *Golden armor.* Around here, that could mean only one thing.

The so-called Bloody Spaniard had sent him here to kill Longarm.

But why? What did the Spaniard have against him? How did the Spaniard even know who he was?

Longarm was more convinced than ever that the spectral, glowing figure in armor wasn't a ghost. A ghost would have no need to hire a gunman. He would just walk through walls and scare his victims to death.

The exchange of gunshots on the second floor drew plenty of attention from the crowd down in the barroom. Mere instants after the gunman's death rattle sounded, a couple of bartenders carrying sawed-off shotguns appeared at the head of the stairs, followed by several curious customers. One of the bartenders leveled his scattergun at Longarm and said, "Hold it right there, mister!"

"Take it easy, old son," drawled Longarm. He slid his Colt back in its holster and straightened, keeping his hands in plain sight so nobody would get nervous and start shooting.

The bartender who had ordered him to hold it was the same one who had poured the drinks for him downstairs, earlier in the evening, and brought him his food at the table. "Mr. Parker?" he said. "What the hell's going on? Who's that fella?"

"I don't rightly know." Longarm prodded the corpse's shoulder with a boot toe. "I was sort of hoping somebody could tell me. All I know is that he was about to bust into my room and start shooting. He didn't know I wasn't in there."

Putting it into words like that gave Longarm even more to ponder. Whoever had sent the gunman after him knew that he had taken a room for the night here on the second floor of the Deuces. They even knew which room it was. But they didn't know he had left the saloon to tend to his horse. Somebody had spied on him and Lady Arabella when she brought him up here, then immediately gone in search of someone to carry out the murder. That was the only way things made sense.

And the theory didn't account for the gunman's last words at all. *Golden armor,* Longarm thought again. For the time being, he wasn't going to say anything about that.

"Custis!" The exclamation came from Lady Arabella Winthrop, who pushed through the crowd on the stairs with an anxious expression on her face. When she saw Longarm standing there apparently unharmed, she looked a bit relieved, but she asked anyway, "Are you all right, Custis?"

Longarm nodded. "I'm fine," he told her. "Just a mite puzzled why this fella wanted me dead."

"I don't understand."

The bartender said, "Mr. Parker caught that man trying to break into his room. Said it looked like the fella meant to drygulch him."

"My God! That's terrible." Lady Arabella came closer to Longarm. "I'm so sorry, Custis. I don't know how such a thing could have happened."

"Maybe he just meant to rob me," said Longarm with a shrug. "He might not have started shooting if I hadn't thrown down on him first."

Even though he didn't believe that for a second, it sounded plausible. He supposed there was even a faint chance it could be true. That didn't explain the "golden armor" business, though, and he was convinced that was one of the keys to the whole thing.

"I sent someone for the sheriff," said Lady Arabella. "He ought to be here soon."

Sure enough, Sheriff Thurston came lumbering up the stairs a few minutes later. By that time, the bartenders had shooed all the bystanders back down into the main room, leaving Longarm and Lady Arabella alone in the upstairs hallway with the dead man.

Thurston grimaced when he saw the corpse. "Two dead fellers in one night," he complained. "When I signed on for this job, I never knew it was gonna be so dad-blasted much work."

Longarm's jaw tightened. Thurston seemed to be a pretty sorry excuse for a lawman, and as a star packer himself, Longarm couldn't abide anybody who wore the badge but didn't take the job seriously. The lack of an effective lawman was probably one reason so much hell was popping in this part of the Panhandle.

Longarm forced himself not to show that reaction. He said, "Sorry, Sheriff. When this hombre started shooting at me, I didn't have time to do much of anything except shoot back at him."

Thurston waved a pudgy hand. "I reckon it ain't your fault. Hell, a man's got the right to defend hisself when somebody tries to rob him." The sheriff looked down at the corpse. "I never seen him before, but he looks like a typical hardcase."

Longarm nodded. "Yeah, just some drifting owlhoot, I reckon." It was best to let the sheriff think that—for now, anyway.

Thurston sighed. "Barney Oglesby is gonna be mighty busy tonight. I'll go let him know about this one."

When the sheriff was gone, Lady Arabella said to Longarm, "I'd really like to make this up to you some way, Custis."

34

"It ain't your fault," Longarm told her again.

"Still, the least I can do is not charge you for your room tonight. You'll allow me to make amends to that extent, won't you?"

"Sure, if it'll make you happy," said Longarm. "It ain't like I'm rolling in *dinero.*"

"Well, for tonight—and at breakfast in the morning, before you ride out to the Box B—you won't need any money. Everything is on the house." She took one last glance at the dead man and shuddered.

The undertaker and his helpers showed up a few minutes later to haul off the corpse. A swamper came from downstairs to mop up the puddle of blood as best he could. Longarm figured the carpet runner was ruined, though.

He retrieved his saddlebags and rifle from the rear hallway and went into his room. It was comfortably furnished with a bed, dressing table, wardrobe, and a couple of straight chairs. The dressing table had a basin and a pitcher of water on it, as well as the lamp, and a clean, porcelain thunder mug was tucked away under the bed. Yellow curtains hung over the single window, and a thick rug lay on the floor next to the bed. Longarm figured he could spend a mighty comfortable night here, as long as he didn't think too much about the fact that he had killed a man right outside the door.

He leaned the Winchester in a corner, hung the saddlebags over the footboard of the bed, and sat down to take off his boots. When he had them off, he unbuttoned his shirt and was about to peel it off when a quiet knock sounded on the door.

Longarm stepped to the foot of the bed and snagged the Colt from its holster. He moved to the door, called, "Who is it?" and quickly stepped to the side just in case somebody fired a load of buckshot through the thin panel.

Instead of a shotgun blast, a soft voice replied, "It's Arabella."

She hadn't used her title, Longarm noted. That probably meant she wasn't feeling very formal. When he opened the door and saw how she was dressed, he knew she wasn't feeling formal at all. She wore a flowing robe of some black, sheer material. Under it, clearly revealed, was a long gown of black silk that clung lovingly to the curves of her body. The gown was cut low enough so that the upper halves of her breasts were visible. Firm, creamy globes of woman flesh, they rode high and proud on her chest. Longarm saw the hard nipples poking out against the clinging fabric of the gown. He lowered his gaze from the jutting breasts over the flat plane of her belly and the swooping curves of her hips and thighs. Black slippers peeked out from under the hem of the long gown.

She had taken down her hair so that it cascaded in raven waves around her head and shoulders. She shook it back a little as she asked, "Do you like what you see, Custis?"

"Very much," said Longarm. "That *is* a bottle of brandy in your hand, isn't it?"

"I meant—" she began as she lifted the bottle, but then she stopped and smiled. "You're having a bit of sport with me, aren't you?"

"I sure as Hades hope I'm about to," Longarm replied with a grin.

"Well, let me in. I don't do this sort of thing very often, you know, and I don't want anyone coming along and seeing me like this."

Longarm stepped back. She brushed past him, filling his senses with a tantalizing scent that wafted from her hair. He closed the door and turned, and she came into his arms, still holding the bottle of brandy and a couple of glasses.

"I don't want anyone seeing me like this except you, Custis," she whispered as she tilted her head back to look up into his face. Her red lips were soft and inviting. Long-arm answered the invitation by bringing his mouth down on hers in a hot, searching kiss. Her body molded to his, her breasts flattening against his broad chest. He cupped one hand behind her neck and slid the other one down her back to her hips as her lips parted and he slipped his tongue between them.

When they finally broke the kiss, he said, "Did you plan on drinking that brandy before . . ."

"After," said Lady Arabella Winthrop. "Definitely after."

Chapter 5

Since he was half-undressed already and she wasn't wearing much to start with, it didn't take long to finish the job of getting both of them nude. Longarm turned down the wick on the lamp, and in the soft amber glow that it gave off, Arabella was even more lovely. They sank back on the bed, and as she lay on top of him and began to kiss his nipples, she murmured, "You must think I'm a terribly wanton woman."

"Not at all," Longarm assured her. Wanton, maybe, he thought, but there was sure as hell nothing terrible about her.

"A proper English noblewoman would never go to bed with a man she's known for only a few hours." She slid down his body until she knelt above his groin. Wrapping both hands around the massive pole of male flesh that jutted up from his groin, she leaned over and sent her tongue slithering hotly around its crown. "And she would certainly never do that. An Englishwoman is much too reserved for such behavior as this."

She opened her mouth wider and took the whole head of his shaft into it. Her raven-tressed head bobbed slightly as she began to suck his thick root.

Longarm rested his head on the pillow and closed his eyes, luxuriating in the sheer pleasure she was giving him. With the part of his brain that was still functioning, he thought about all the Englishwomen he had known over the years. Sure, some of them had been a mite reserved— at first—but almost without fail, once they got over that they were every bit as passionate as their American sisters. Of course, what Arabella was doing to him now was more French in nature . . .

She was good at it, too. His shaft swelled until she could barely get both hands around it, and just the head was enough to fill her mouth. She reached down with one hand and cupped the heavy sacs beneath it, gently rolling them back and forth in her palm.

If she kept doing what she was doing for much longer, he would have no choice but to unleash his climax in the hot, wet cavern of her mouth. She stopped, though, and lifted her head to smile at him. "My word, there's a lot of you, Custis!" she said. "How in the world did you manage to acquire an instrument of such magnitude?"

"Just lucky, I reckon," said Longarm. "I was born with it."

"Well, I certainly owe a debt of thanks to whatever ancestor of yours passed it down to you." Still cradling his manhood in her hands, she moved over him, poising herself above the burgeoning shaft. Slowly, she lowered her hips, guiding him into position. The head of his organ touched the folds of heated flesh at the opening between her legs. She moved it back and forth, all along the slit, letting him feel how drenched she was.

Then she settled down more, taking him in a bit at a time. Inch by maddening inch she enveloped him. The heat of her sheath was incredible, and it was all Longarm could do not to thrust up from the mattress with his hips and imbed himself all the way inside her. He was willing to allow her to set the pace, though . . . just as long as she didn't take *too* much time getting him inside her.

He could do some teasing of his own, he decided. He reached up and cupped her breasts, using his thumbs to stroke the hard brown nipples that stood out in dark circles against the milky flesh around them. "Oh, my dear . . ." she murmured, and he knew she liked what he was doing to her. He twirled the nipples between thumb and forefinger, and her breath began to come harder and faster.

"Oh, the devil with it!" she suddenly exclaimed, and she let her weight down on him. His hips arched involuntarily. She gasped as he penetrated her all the way, sheathing the entire throbbing length of his manhood inside her feminine core.

Longarm tightened his grip on her breasts to steady her as he began thrusting in and out of her. Her hips pumped back and forth as she met his thrusts with her own that were every bit as eager. She rested her hands on his chest, bracing herself as she rode him.

He was deep, deep inside her, filling her. "Custis, oh, Custis!" she panted. He shifted his hands to her hips to hold her on. She was bucking so hard he was afraid she was going to come right off of him if she wasn't careful.

Then she slammed down against him and he drove up into her, and both of them froze while he was at his deepest penetration yet. A massive shudder went through him as he began to empty himself into her. A matching shudder marked her own culmination. Longarm's seed erupted in thick, white-hot jets that mixed with her fluids and soaked them both, inside and out, as she overflowed.

With a groan of utter satisfaction, she sagged forward and sprawled on top of him. He slid his arms around her and held her tightly.

"That was incredible, Custis," she murmured after a moment.

Longarm patted her rump lightly and said, "I couldn't agree more, Lady Arabella."

She lifted her head from his chest and looked down into his eyes. "You don't have to use my title," she told him. "I think we're well beyond that stage now."

"You don't mind that I'm a commoner?" asked Longarm with a mischievous grin.

She laughed and wiggled her hips. He was still semi-erect inside her, and her movement made his thick shaft give a little jump. "There's nothing common about you, my friend."

They lay on the bed for a while longer, stroking each other. Finally, Arabella got up and pulled her gown on. She uncorked the brandy and poured it in the stemmed, wide-bowled snifters she had brought up with her. Then she sat on the foot of the bed while Longarm propped his back against the headboard. They swirled the liquor in the glasses and sipped from them.

"You know," Arabella said slowly, "you don't seem much like the usual grub line rider to me, Custis. You're too intelligent."

"Just because a fella punches cows don't mean he can't be smart."

"No, of course not. But there's also the way you handled that man who tried to break in here and ambush you. Most cowboys I've seen aren't quite that handy with a gun."

Longarm felt a faint stirring of unease. Arabella was on the verge of seeing through his pose. Should he tell her who he really was, or should he continue the masquerade and deny what she was saying? He felt that he could trust her, and he knew he was a pretty good judge of character. He had to be, or he wouldn't have stayed alive so long in such a dangerous profession.

On the other hand, he hated to abandon the role he was playing, even with one person, until he had discovered everything he could about the perilous shroud of outlawry that lay over the Panhandle.

He shook his head. "I was just lucky, I reckon. And I've practiced a mite with a six-gun over the years."

Arabella took another sip of the brandy and looked at him over the rim of the glass. "I imagine you have," she said quietly. Abruptly, she upended the snifter and drank the rest of the liquor. "I won't press you on the matter. It's really none of my business."

He saw that he might have offended her. He regretted that, but there was nothing he could do about it.

"As I said, I don't do things of this sort very often," she went on as she reached for the bottle. "I indulged a momentary whim, and it led to some wonderful moments of passion. But that's all it was, a whim. I've no claim on you, Custis. You're free to ride on and take whatever job you like."

"I figure I'll be punching cows for Charley Barfield," he said.

Arabella splashed more brandy in her glass, drank it down. "Remember what I said about Arch Kellman having a reputation with a gun? I believe Charley suspects he knows who is behind the rustling, and soon he's going to be ready to take action. I expect that a man such as yourself would play a part in that action."

Longarm frowned. "Are you saying that Barfield's working himself up for a war of some sort, and you think he really hired me for my gun?"

"It's possible." Arabella came to her feet. "But I've said too much. I survive here in Tascosa by providing entertainment for the men from all the ranches in the area. In order to do that, I have to remain neutral and not take sides in any clashes. I intend to continue doing just that. Good night, Custis."

"Good night," said Longarm.

She thumped the half-empty bottle on the dressing table. "I'll leave this. On the house, like everything else."

She snatched up her robe and swept out of the room

before he could frame a reply. The door closed softly behind her. Longarm frowned at the panel before he leaned over and blew out the flame in the lamp.

Arabella had given him a lot to think about. He wasn't surprised that it was quite a while before he fell asleep.

He awoke the next morning feeling fairly refreshed physically, but his thoughts weren't any clearer than they had been when he drifted off the night before. When he dressed and went downstairs for breakfast, he saw no sign of Arabella. He supposed she was sleeping in this morning.

The saloon was almost empty. One man, a professional gambler by the looks of him, sat at a table dealing a desultory hand of solitaire. Another man, wearing a store clerk's apron, stood at the bar with a mug of beer. An eye-opener before starting the day's work, Longarm supposed. Only one bartender was on duty at this time of day, and he was a stranger. Evidently he had been given Longarm's description, though, because he nodded and said, "Mornin', Mr. Parker. I'll have the cook rustle you up some breakfast."

"Much obliged," said Longarm. "And if you've got any coffee boiling, I could use a cup."

"Right away."

Longarm sat down at one of the empty tables. Within minutes, he had a cup of steaming black Arbuckle's in front of him. Not long after that, the bartender brought a platter of food from the kitchen. Longarm dug into the meal, enjoying the thick slices of ham, fried eggs, hash browns, and biscuits and sorghum. The strong black coffee did a good job of washing it all down.

By the time he was finished with the food, Arabella still hadn't put in an appearance. He said to the bartender, "Have you seen your boss this morning?"

"Lady Arabella?" The man shook his head. "She hardly

ever wakes up before noon. Usually it's one or two o'clock in the afternoon."

Longarm frowned. He would have liked to see her again, if for no other reason than to find out if relations between them were still strained. But Charley Barfield was expecting him out at the ranch this morning, and Longarm didn't want to waste the opportunity to find out more about what was going on around here. From what Arabella had said, Barfield thought he had at least an idea of who was behind the rustling.

Longarm drained the last of the coffee from the cup and got to his feet. "Tell the lady that I appreciate all of her kindnesses," he said to the bartender.

"Yes, sir, I'll do that."

"And let her know, too, that I'll be around. I expect I'll be seeing her again."

"Sure. I'll tell her."

"You know the Box B?" asked Longarm.

"Charley Barfield's spread? Of course. I know most of the ranchers around here."

"Can you tell me how to get out to Barfield's place?"

The bartender nodded and gave him directions. The Box B lay southwest of Tascosa and was made up of thousands of acres that sprawled along the border between Texas and New Mexico Territory. From time to time, the state government of Texas and the territorial government of New Mexico squabbled over exactly where that boundary line lay. As far as Longarm knew, no such political arguments were going on at the moment.

He left the Deuces and walked down the street to the livery stable where he'd left his horse. The animal had been grained and watered and seemed frisky, ready to get out and stretch its legs. The hostler offered to saddle the horse, but Longarm did that himself, out of habit. He liked to make sure everything was secure before he set off on a ride. When he was satisfied, he swung up into the saddle, dug a coin from his pocket, and flipped it to the hostler. "Much obliged to you for taking good care of this cayuse," he said to the man.

The elderly hostler caught the coin, bit into it, and nodded approvingly at the marks his teeth left in the gold. "Come back anytime," he told Longarm with a grin.

Longarm left Tascosa and rode toward the New Mexico line, angling southwest from the settlement. The terrain was mostly flat, with an occasional shallow, rolling hill. The ground was covered with bunch grass and dotted with clumps of stubby mesquite trees. Gullies slashed across the landscape, like giant fingers had clawed them there. Most of the arroyos were dry most of the year, though rainstorms sometimes sent water flowing through them. A few had springs in them that kept trickles of water moving along except in the most arid months.

When Longarm lifted his eyes to the western horizon, he saw a low line of blue that marked a range of mountains. Those rounded peaks were over the border in New Mexico Territory, he knew. A man could see a long, long way out here in West Texas... The problem was that there wasn't a whole hell of a lot to see.

But it was good cattle country, and the vast ranches that had grown up here in the past ten or fifteen years took advantage of that fact. Those spreads ran massive herds on their range. Once millions of buffalo had grazed here. Now longhorns had taken their place.

As his horse jogged along, Longarm realized he wasn't that far off the trail he had taken the night before. That meant he was fairly close to the spot where he had seen Barfield's men chasing that glowing, spectral figure.

He had intended to have a look at the place where the Bloody Spaniard had disappeared. Now was as good a time as any, Longarm decided. That wouldn't delay him long enough to make Barfield worry about him.

He angled his horse north by west. He wasn't sure exactly where the chase had taken place. This part of the country was short on landmarks to start with, since so much of it was flat and featureless. And it had been dark when he'd seen the Spaniard and then had his run-in with Arch Kellman and the rest of Barfield's riders. But he thought he was going the right direction, and after a while he became sure of it. He came across the tracks of a lot of horses, moving in a hurry. Charley Barfield and the others had left those tracks as they were chasing the Spaniard, thought Longarm.

He followed the tracks, found the spot where the riders had stopped, regrouped, and then turned toward Tascosa. Circling, he found his own tracks coming in from the west.

He found, as well, a single set of hoofprints leading northwest. Longarm reined in and frowned at them. Those were the ones left by the Spaniard's horse. Had to be, he thought. So the horse was flesh and blood, whether the rider was a ghost or not.

Longarm still didn't believe that. A ghost rider would need a ghost horse, wouldn't he? That seemed logical. The hoofprints were just one more indication that the Bloody Spaniard was real, not a phantom.

He followed the tracks as they wound through some clumps of mesquite. The growth was thicker here, and that might have helped the Spaniard give his pursuers the slip.

Suddenly, Longarm reined in with a sharp tug. Without warning as he rounded some of the mesquites, he found himself on the lip of an arroyo. A narrow path ran down into the dry wash. Longarm grinned as he looked at it. He knew now how the Spaniard had disappeared. The hombre had simply ridden down into this arroyo and followed it for a ways. He might have even stopped and removed the armor. If Longarm's half-formed theory that the armor was painted with some sort of luminous substance was correct, the so-called Spaniard could have hidden it, or at least covered it up somehow, and ridden off into the night, practically invisible in the shadows.

Of course, there were still the questions of just who was inside that armor and how was he connected with the tide of lawlessness washing over the Panhandle, but Longarm felt like he was making a little progress anyway.

He wasn't nearly as satisfied with himself a moment later, though, as he heard the distinctive sound of a gun being cocked and a man's voice saying harshly, "Do not move, señor, or I will blow a hole right through you. This I swear."

Chapter 6

Longarm did as he was told, though it rankled him. But only a fool ignored such a command when it was backed up with a cocked and leveled gun. He was willing to bide his time and see who had gotten the drop on him.

He didn't have to wait long. With a rattle of hooves against the dry ground, a man rode up alongside him, staying several yards away so that he was out of easy reach. He pointed an old Dragoon Colt at Longarm, and the muzzle of the cap-and-ball revolver looked as big around as the mouth of a cannon. The man's hand didn't shake, either, as it supported the heavy weapon.

"Take your gun out carefully and drop it on the ground, señor."

Longarm still didn't move. He said coolly, "I reckon I'd rather not do that. Might get sand in the barrel and the action, and then I'd have a chore cleaning it."

The barrel of the Dragoon quivered a little, but it was from anger, not fatigue on the part of the young man wielding it. "Do as I tell you!" the man ordered sharply. "Do you think I will not kill you?"

"That's right," said Longarm. "I think you won't kill

me." His voice was calm and strong, but he knew he was wagering a lot on that opinion.

His life, in fact.

But his keen eyes had made a quick study of the youngster holding the gun on him, and he judged that the hombre wasn't the sort to gun down a fella in cold blood. No more than twenty years old, his olive-skinned face was clean-shaven, his eyes dark and quick. He wore the tight trousers with flared legs and the short charro jacket favored by Mexican vaqueros. A broad-brimmed, high-crowned sombrero made of brown felt sat atop thick, crisp, black hair. His horse was a good-looking bay, with an old, plain, but well-cared-for saddle. Nothing about the young man was fancy, but he carried himself with a proud air anyway.

He glared darkly at Longarm, but before he could say anything else, a new voice called, "Ramon! Ramon, what are you doing? Put down that gun!"

This voice belonged to a female, which came as a surprise to Longarm. He hadn't expected to run into a gal out here. But he hadn't expected to be threatened by a young Mexican gun-thrower, either. He turned his head as he heard more hoofbeats approaching rapidly.

The newcomer was dressed much like the young man, except that her hat was flat-crowned and had a smaller brim. It was black instead of brown, too. She was a couple of years older than the youngster called Ramon, and there was a definite family resemblance between them. They were brother and sister, Longarm decided.

The woman rode a chestnut mare with white markings on its nose and chest. Around her slender waist was strapped a gunbelt with a holster thonged to her thigh. She carried a smaller pistol than her brother, its ivory handle jutting up from the holster. She also looked mad as hell.

"Did you not hear me?" she demanded as she reined in

a few yards away from Longarm and the young man. "Put away your gun!"

"This is none of your business, Rosa!" he blazed back at her. "I have caught this gringo rustler on our range, and I intend to deal with him properly!"

"Just a couple of points, old son," drawled Longarm. "One, I ain't a rustler, and two, I ain't of a mind to be dealt with, if you get my drift. Not without doing some dealing of my own."

The young woman's presence complicated things. Riding up and giving orders the way she had done had wounded Ramon's pride. Now the youngster might feel honor bound to make a showdown out of this confrontation. Ramon's attention had strayed with his sister's arrival, and Longarm felt fairly confident he could close the distance between them and slap that Dragoon aside before Ramon could fire. But there was a chance lead could go flying around anyway, and somebody could be hurt. Longarm didn't want that.

"Tell you what, though," he went on. "I'll give my gun to your big sis here. That satisfy you?"

Ramon glared at him again. "How do you know this is my sister?"

"Well, she ain't old enough to be your mama, and the two of you look a heap alike."

The young woman kneed her horse closer to Longarm and held out her hand. "Give me your gun, as you suggested. And Ramon, please put yours away."

Making it a request like that allowed Ramon to save face. The gal probably knew her brother pretty well, thought Longarm. Using his left hand and being slow and careful-like about it, he drew the Colt from its holster and extended it butt-first to her. As she took it, Ramon reluctantly holstered the Dragoon. Still glaring at Longarm, he said, "You claim you are not a rustler. If this is so, what are you doing on our land?"

"Didn't know it was your range," replied Longarm. Omitting any mention of the Bloody Spaniard and the chase that had taken place here the previous night, he went on, "I was just riding out to the Box B."

That was the wrong thing to say, he realized as soon as the words were out of his mouth. Ramon's face darkened even more with anger, and his sister Rosa frowned. Ramon spat on the ground between his horse and Longarm's and then began cursing in Spanish.

As Ramon reached for his gun again, Rosa jerked the reins and sent her horse forward, quickly getting between her brother and Longarm. She was upset, that much was obvious, but she still didn't want any gunplay if it could be avoided.

In swift Spanish, she ordered Ramon to back off. Then she swung around toward Longarm and said, "You associate with rustlers, but you are not a rustler yourself? This is what you would have us believe?"

Longarm was a little lost here. He hadn't heard any talk in Tascosa about Charley Barfield and his men being suspected of wrongdoing. True, according to Lady Arabella, the Box B hadn't been hit by the raiders, but that didn't have to mean anything except that Barfield had been lucky so far.

"If the Box B is responsible for any widelooping, I don't know a thing about it," said Longarm honestly.

"What is your business with Señor Barfield? I know such a question is impolite, but Ramon and I must know."

Longarm smiled grimly. "I'm going to work for him. He's got a riding job open since one of his men was killed in Tascosa last night."

Rosa's dark eyes widened slightly in surprise. "Killed? Who?"

"A young cowboy called Rance."

Ramon said, "I know him. He was no better than any of those other gringo thieves."

"Hush, Ramon!" exclaimed Rosa. "Do not speak ill of the dead. You know better."

"I feel no sympathy for any gringo. They are all thieves, Rosa. *You* know *that*."

This youngster was carrying around quite a grudge, thought Longarm. He didn't know why Ramon felt that way, and at the moment he didn't particularly care. What he wanted to know was why these two thought Barfield and his men were rustlers.

"I reckon you must have a spread around here," he said, "since you claim this is your range."

Ramon's temper flared again. "It *is* our range! And no damned gringo will steal it!"

Rosa held out a hand to quiet him. "Yes, this is our ranch," she said to Longarm. "Our headquarters are west of here, near the border with New Mexico Territory. Our ranch is small compared to most of the others here in the Panhandle—"

"But we will fight for it!" Ramon broke in. "Make no mistake about that, gringo!"

Longarm sighed. "You know, old son, the way you say that is getting a mite tiresome. It's plain to see you've gotten crossways with some folks in the past, but I never stole nothing from you, and I don't figure to start now. And since I'm about twice your age I reckon you ought to mind your manners and respect your elders."

A hard edge had crept into his voice as he spoke. Ramon flushed but didn't say anything in response to the rebuke.

"Clearly, there has been a misunderstanding," said Rosa. "Our apologies, señor. Perhaps introductions are in order. I am Rosalinda Hernandez, and as you surmised, this is my brother Ramon."

"Custis Parker," said Longarm, continuing to use the alias. "I'd say it was a pleasure, ma'am, but to tell the truth, so far it ain't been much of one."

"Perhaps we can remedy that. If you will accompany us to our ranch . . . ?"

"Rosa!" Ramon burst out. "You invite this man to our home?"

At least that time the young fella hadn't called him a gringo, thought Longarm dryly.

"I accept your invitation, ma'am," he said. That would delay him even more in reaching the Box B, but a visit to the Hernandez ranch might give him more information about what was going on in these parts. Clearly there was bad blood between these two and Charley Barfield, and that needed some explaining.

"I will keep your gun for the time being," said Rosa.

Longarm nodded in acceptance of the condition. The butt of his Winchester was within easy reach where it protruded from its saddle boot, but if she chose to ignore that fact, he could, too.

"Ride on ahead, Ramon," she went on. "Tell Alejandro that we are having a guest."

Ramon leaned over and spat again. "Guest," he repeated, and in his mouth the word sounded obscene. But he did as his sister told him, whirling his bay around and sending the horse leaping into a gallop. He headed west and vanished within moments.

"My apologies, Señor Parker," said Rosa as she and Longarm rode at a slower pace after Ramon. "The veins of my brother carry the hot, impulsive blood of our ancestors."

"I reckon Spanish folks ain't the only ones who are a mite hair-triggered," replied Longarm. "I've run into plenty of people of all races who are too quick to jump the gun."

"You are generous in your forgiveness."

"You sound like you've decided I ain't a rustler after all, even though I know Charley Barfield."

Rosa's voice was taut as she said, "I am not as convinced as Ramon that Señor Barfield is to blame for the lawlessness that plagues this land. But I am not certain of his innocence, either."

"I've known the hombre less than a day, myself," said Longarm. "He didn't strike me as an owlhoot, but I could be wrong about him."

"Whether he steals our cattle or not, he does not like it that Ramon and I are here. That much I know."

Big ranchers often held small, greasy-sack outfits in contempt, Longarm knew. That might be the case here if the Hernandez range was considerably smaller than the Box B. As he rode along next to Rosa, he asked, "How many head do you run?"

"About five hundred. Compared to the other ranches in the Panhandle, the Eagle is nothing. But it is everything to us."

"That's the name of your spread? The Eagle Ranch?"

"*Sí.* And our brand is like this." A slender, graceful hand moved in the air, tracing the shape of an eagle's wings spread in flight. Longarm had been below the border enough to know that Mexican haciendas often had pretty, even poetic names, though their brands tended to look like a skillet full of snakes writhing over a hot fire.

"How long have you been here in the Panhandle?"

"Two years. Ever since . . . ever since we had to leave New Mexico Territory."

Longarm heard the catch in her voice and glanced over. He saw pain, resentment, and loss lurking in her eyes. "What happened?" he asked softly. "Not that it's any of my business, mind you, but if you want to talk about it . . ."

For a second he thought Rosa wasn't going to respond, but then she said, "My family held one of the old land grants from the king of Spain. For centuries we had one of the finest ranches in Nuevo Mexico. According to the Treaty of Guadalupe Hidalgo, the land grant should have remained in force. But some greedy American ranchers used their money and influence and persuaded a judge to set it aside so that they could move in on what had been our land."

Longarm frowned. He had been involved in several land grant cases and knew something about them. "That don't hardly sound right," he said. "Seems to me like you could have appealed that decision."

"Perhaps. But in the meantime men with guns came to force us off our hacienda. Ramon wanted to fight, but my father would not allow it. He was more concerned that no harm come to Ramon or me. But he was a proud man, a very proud man, and to be humiliated that way . . ." Rosa shook her head. "He died not long after. I am convinced it was a broken spirit that killed him."

Longarm rode along in silence for a few minutes. He could understand why Ramon Hernandez hated all gringos. It sounded like he and his family had gotten a raw deal, all right.

Rosa resumed the story. "After my father passed away, Ramon and I were the only ones left. Our mother died many years ago, and none of our brothers and sisters lived through childhood. It was a hard existence, even on a successful ranch."

Longarm nodded. "Living on the frontier has always been a challenge, I reckon. Probably always will be."

"*Sí.* I had promised my father that I would look after Ramon, so we left New Mexico Territory and came here to Texas. I knew if he stayed there, sooner or later there would be trouble with the men who took our land. We had some money from the sale of our father's cattle, so we used it to buy a small ranch here in the Panhandle. The man who owned it wanted to move on, because he had lost his wife to a fever. He was not that fond of selling out to a couple of *greasers* . . ." Her mouth twisted as she repeated the epithet the cattleman must have used. "But

56

he wanted the money. So now we have the Eagle Ranch, and we struggle to make it a good place to live."

"But you've been hit by rustlers, you say?"

"Over the past three months, we have lost more than a hundred head. In a herd the size of ours, that is a significant loss, Señor Parker. We try to guard the cattle, but there are only Ramon and myself to watch them, along with Alejandro Carranza, who was my father's majordomo. We do the best we can, but . . ." She shrugged wordlessly, the gesture eloquent in itself.

Longarm knew what she meant. With only three hands to patrol the ranch, and one of them a woman, the Eagle would be easy pickings for a gang of wideloopers. In a way, the Hernandez siblings were lucky they had any cattle left at all.

"What makes you think Charley Barfield had anything to do with the stock you lost?" he asked.

"His range borders ours to the south. It would be easy for his men to slip across and cut out some of our animals."

"Maybe so, but somebody else could do the same thing," Longarm pointed out. "Wouldn't have to be Barfield and his bunch."

"It is not only that. One of his riders, a man called Kellman, warned us that there would be trouble if we did not give up our ranch. I think Señor Barfield wants our land for himself, just like the men in New Mexico wanted our hacienda there. Here, though, he plans to wipe us out, rather than using the courts."

Longarm had a hard time believing that Charley Barfield would try to smash his neighbors like that so he could grab their land. But, he reminded himself, he didn't know Barfield all that well. And he had no trouble believing that Arch Kellman would threaten Ramon and Rosa Hernandez.

"Maybe I can talk to Barfield for you," he said. "Could be things ain't as bad as you think."

"I doubt if talking will do any good, but I appreciate the offer, Señor Parker."

Longarm was about to ask her if she knew anything about a night rider in glowing golden armor, when he heard a series of popping noises up ahead somewhere. He stiffened in the saddle, and so did Rosa.

"Is that—" she gasped.

"Gunfire," said Longarm. Like it or not, hell was loose in the Panhandle again.

Chapter 7

Longarm sent his horse leaping forward, racing toward the sound of the shots. Rosa was right behind him, and he didn't waste time or breath shouting for her to stay back. He knew she wouldn't pay any attention to him. She would be thinking the same thing Longarm was.

Her brother Ramon was up there somewhere, and it was a mighty good bet that he was mixed up somehow in that shooting.

Sound could travel a long way in the dry air over the flat prairie. Longarm wasn't sure how close the shots were. He didn't think it would take long to reach the scene of the trouble, though, and he was right. After a few minutes of hard riding, he sighted some puffs of smoke in the air ahead. That was powder smoke, he told himself, coming from the guns of the men who were carrying on what now sounded like a small-scale battle.

He reined in, not wanting to go blundering into the middle of the fracas until he knew exactly what was going on. He pulled the Winchester from its sheath and then hipped around in the saddle and motioned for Rosa to slow down. She was about twenty yards behind him, his long-legged mount having outdistanced her pony.

She hauled back on the reins and brought her horse to a stop. "Stay there!" Longarm called to her, hoping she would heed the warning. He turned back toward the battle and walked his horse forward, guiding the animal with his knees, the rifle held ready in his hands.

After a moment he was able to make out what was going on. He spotted a dark shape on the ground near some mesquites and recognized it as the bay gelding that Ramon had been riding. There was movement on the far side of the horse. The crown of a brown felt sombrero poked into the air. Instantly, rifles cracked and pistols barked from the mesquite thicket, and the headgear jerked out of sight, ripped by ambush lead.

Longarm read the scene as easily as he would have words. Bushwhackers had lurked in the cover of those mesquites as Ramon rode by. The gunmen had opened up on him, dropping his mount with a fatal wound. Ramon was still alive, though, and now he hunkered behind the dead horse, pinned down by the fire of the men who wanted to kill him. Out in the open like that, if he stood up to make a run for it, he would be riddled before he got ten feet.

Despite his desperate situation, the youngster still had some fight in him. As Longarm watched, Ramon thrust the barrel of the Dragoon over the horse's corpse and pulled the trigger. The old revolver exploded with a dull boom and a puff of smoke, sending a heavy lead ball through the thicket where his ambushers hid. Ramon was outnumbered, though, and he couldn't fight off a whole gang of killers with an old cap-and-ball Dragoon.

It was time for Longarm to take a hand in this game.

He swung down from the saddle and tugged on the reins until the horse knelt and lay over on its side. A live horse wasn't as good cover as a dead one, but a live one could carry a man out of trouble a whole heap faster. This mount was rented from a livery stable over in Raton, and

Longarm didn't know how well he would stand up to guns going off around him, but there was only one way to find out.

Tossing his hat aside, Longarm sprawled on his belly behind the horse and slid the Winchester over its quivering flank. He saw the bushwhackers only as indistinct shapes among the mesquites, but he had a better angle at them than Ramon did. Drawing a bead on one of the shapes, Longarm squeezed the trigger. The rifle blasted and the horse flinched, but it didn't leap up. Longarm worked the Winchester's lever, jacking another shell into the chamber. Quickly, he shifted his aim and fired again and then again.

In a double handful of heartbeats, he raked the mesquite thicket with half a dozen slugs. As the echoes of the shots rolled away, Longarm heard startled shouts and curses. The men hiding in the scrubby trees were aware of this new threat, and some of them swung around to face it. Several shots rapped out. Bullets whined over Longarm's head.

He glanced over his shoulder toward the spot where he had left Rosa, hoping she was far enough back to be out of danger. His jaw tightened in surprise as he saw that she wasn't even anywhere in sight. Maybe she had retreated a long way from the fight, he told himself, or maybe she had gone for help.

A second later, as he heard the swift rataplan of hoofbeats, he knew that neither of those theories was correct. He lifted his head and peered off to the right, toward the sound of the racing horse. Rosa came into sight, galloping hard toward the mesquite thicket, circling toward the far side of it. She had the pistol in her hand. The gun cracked wickedly as she peppered the mesquites with lead.

Rosa's unexpected appearance must have taken the bushwhackers by surprise. They found themselves under attack from three directions now as their ambush blew up

61

in their faces. But Longarm knew that he and Rosa and
Ramon still were outgunned, more than likely, so they had
to press their advantage while they had the chance. He
came up on his knees beside the trembling horse and
opened fire again, slamming shots from the Winchester
into the thicket as fast as he could pull the trigger and
work the rifle's lever.

Off to the left, Ramon's Dragoon continued to boom,
the heavier reports counterpointing the sharp cracks of
Rosa's revolver. Such concentrated fire could last only
seconds, Longarm knew, before he and the two Hernandez siblings ran out of ammunition and would have to
reload.

The bushwhackers didn't have the patience to wait out
such a withering attack, however. Suddenly, three men on
horseback burst out of the mesquite thicket, blazing away
with handguns as they fogged it to the south. Longarm
had to dive to the ground behind the horse to avoid being
ventilated by some of the flying lead. He rolled over,
ended up on his belly again, and sent a final shot after the
fleeing bushwhackers. He didn't think he hit any of them,
but at least he hurried them along, he told himself.

He snatched up his hat and then leaned over and
grabbed his horse's reins. The animal climbed to its feet
in response to Longarm's tug. He stepped up into the saddle and heeled the horse into a run toward Ramon.

The youngster swung his gun toward Longarm as the
big lawman approached. "Hold your fire!" he bellowed.
"It's me, Custis Parker!"

Ramon lowered the old revolver. He was pale, and
blood streaked his face. He didn't seem to be badly hurt,
though. He stood up shakily and said, "Rosa! Where is
Rosa?"

Longarm wondered about that himself. He had lost
sight of the young woman as she swept around the mesquite thicket, wielding that pistol like a beautiful avenging

angel. He looked around, hoping to see some sign of her.

A wave of relief washed through him as she appeared, trotting her pony around the mesquites. She still had the gun in her hand as she rode hurriedly over to Longarm and Ramon. She didn't holster it until she reined in. Leaping out of the saddle, she rushed over to her brother and grabbed his shoulders.

"Ramon!" she cried. "Are you all right?"

He nodded. "*Sí.*"

She touched the blood on his face. "You are hurt!"

"A scratch, nothing more," he assured her. "And you?"

"I'm fine." She hugged him fiercely for a second and then turned her head to look at Longarm. "Señor Parker? You are not wounded?"

Longarm grinned. "Nope, I didn't get elected. Not even nominated."

Ramon reached for the trailing reins of Rosa's horse. "I am going after those *bastardos*—"

"No!" Rosa caught hold of his hand. "Let them go, Ramon. We should be grateful that we all survived this fight."

"Not all," said Ramon glumly as he looked down at the stiffening body of his bay.

Longarm reached into his saddlebags, brought out a box of .44–40s, and started thumbing fresh cartridges into his rifle to replace the ones he had fired. He said, "Seems to me there were more than three of those skunks in that thicket. I'm going to have a look around."

"I will go with you," declared Ramon. He seemed to have forgotten his earlier hostility toward Longarm.

Longarm shook his head. "Stay here with your sister. If there's any more trouble, jump on that cayuse of mine and both of you light a shuck out of here." The words came out in a crisp tone of command, and though both Rosa and Ramon looked like they wanted to argue with him, neither of them did.

Keeping the rifle ready for instant use, Longarm walked over to the mesquites and forced his way into the thicket. The branches clawed at him, but he ignored them, pushing the growth aside with the Winchester's barrel. A few minutes of searching turned up what he thought he would find. Two men lay dead among the mesquites, the sandy ground around them dark with spilled blood. Not far away, the horses belonging to the dead bushwhackers were still tied, waiting for owners who would never return to claim them.

Longarm hunkered next to the corpses and studied their faces. If there was anything to what Rosa and Ramon said about Charley Barfield wanting to run them off their ranch, these men might be Box B riders. But Longarm didn't recognize either of them from the night before. That didn't rule out the possibility they might work for Barfield, of course, but at least it didn't point a finger of guilt directly at the burly cattleman. Neither of the horses was branded with a Box B, either. One sported a Three J iron, the other a Rafter M. Those spreads weren't anywhere around here, and likely the animals had gone through more than one owner since leaving the ranches where they were foaled.

Leaving the dead men where they were for the time being, Longarm untied the reins and led the two horses out of the thicket. "You can ride one of these," he said to Ramon. "The gents who owned them won't be needing them anymore."

Rosa shuddered a little. "They are dead?"

"Dead as can be," said Longarm with a nod.

"Could you tell . . . Could you tell if I . . . if I killed them?"

Longarm looked at her. Her hat had slipped back on her head while she was galloping around during the fight, so that it hung behind her from its neck strap. Her hair had been tucked up earlier, but now it fell freely in dark waves around her shoulders. Longarm had known she was pretty when he first saw her. Now he knew that she was beautiful. But her face, lovely as it was, showed the strain she was feeling at the thought she might have ended the life of at least one man.

"Looked to me like rifle fire that did them in," he lied. In truth, he had no idea which of them had killed the bushwhackers, and he wasn't going to dig out the fatal slugs to see. "I reckon I ventilated both of them."

Rosa looked relieved. Ramon, on the other hand, seemed a little disappointed that he hadn't downed at least one of the ambushers. He could just live with that disappointment, thought Longarm wryly.

"The dead men," asked Rosa, "did you know them?"

"Never saw them before."

"I should look and see if I know who they are . . ."

"Stay here," said Ramon. "I will look."

She nodded, willing to let her brother handle the grisly chore. Longarm gave her the reins to hold while he led Ramon back into the thicket.

The youngster looked over the corpses and then shook his head. "I was hoping they would be some of Barfield's men. But I do not know them."

"You sure of that?" asked Longarm.

"Sí. They look like rustlers and gunmen, though."

That was true enough. The two men had the look of typical hardcases, the sort of owlhoots who ran in packs, like wild dogs. Longarm didn't figure to lose any sleep over their deaths.

He and Ramon rejoined Rosa. "When I get to the Box B, I'll see if Barfield will send one of his men to town to let the sheriff know about this," Longarm said as the three of them rode on. Ramon led the extra horse.

The young man snorted contemptuously in response to Longarm's comment. "Sheriff Thurston will not care. All that matters to him is that nothing disturb his eating and his siestas."

"He didn't seem like much of a lawman to me," agreed Longarm, "but I reckon he's all the law the folks around here have got."

"Yes, and that is why rustlers and thieves and killers run loose," said Rosa. "This is a hard land. It will never be a paradise. But it could be so much better a place to live than it is now."

"Maybe one of these days," said Longarm softly. "One of these days . . ."

They rode on, and a short time later they came within sight of the ranch. Rosa pointed out the adobe house and barn and the corrals. Ramon said, "I will ride on and tell Alejandro you are coming, as you said earlier." He spurred out ahead of Longarm and Rosa.

As they rode along at a slower pace, Longarm looked over at Rosa. She hadn't replaced her hat, so her hair was still loose around her face and shoulders, cascading half-way down her back like a dark waterfall. Some of her color had returned, and she seemed to be getting over the horror that had seized her when she thought she had killed a man.

"That was sort of a wild stunt you pulled back there, riding around those mesquites like that," Longarm told her.

She nodded. "I know. But all I could think of was that Ramon was in danger, and I could not stay back and let a stranger risk his life alone to save him."

"You handle a six-shooter pretty well."

"My father made sure I knew how to shoot. He was old-fashioned in many ways and believed that a woman should remain in the home and solve all her problems by smiling and taking care of her man, so that he will take care of her. But Papa could be practical, too. He said that sometimes no man was around, so a woman had to be able to ride and shoot if she had to. I am thankful to *El Señor Dios* that my father taught me as well as he did."

Longarm nodded. He felt a strong instinctive liking for Rosalinda Hernandez, and it wasn't only because she was so attractive. She was smart and levelheaded, too, not to mention courageous when the chips were down.

"Do you know anything about an hombre who rides around at night dressed like one of the old conquistadors?"

He asked the question in a mildly curious tone of voice, but it was still enough to make her jerk her head toward him. "The Bloody Spaniard!" she exclaimed. "Everyone around here knows of him. You have heard about him already?"

"More than that," said Longarm. "I've seen the fella."

"You saw him with your own eyes?"

Longarm nodded. "Back yonder at the place where I first ran into you and your brother. That was last night. Charley Barfield and some of the Box B riders were chasing him."

"Barfield? That makes no sense, Señor Parker. Ramon and I, we have wondered if this so-called Bloody Spaniard is really one of Barfield's men."

"That don't seem likely to me, not after what I saw last night. The Box B was after that hombre in the armor, right enough. You figured he was connected with Barfield because you blame Barfield for the rustling that's been going on, right?"

"*Sí.* If Barfield and his men are really the outlaws, and the Spaniard is working *with* the outlaws, then why would they chase him?" Rosa shook her head. "I do not understand any of this, Señor Parker, but if what you say is true, then Ramon and I must have been wrong about Barfield."

Longarm grinned and tugged at his earlobe. "Don't worry, you ain't the only one who's a mite confused. I'm

67

still trying to puzzle it all out myself." He paused, then added, "You know, some folks say the Spaniard is a ghost."

"There are many stories of ghosts and spirits among my people. Some swear they are true. As for myself . . . I do not know. Somehow, though, I think this Spaniard is flesh and blood—and I think he is a gringo."

"What makes you say that?"

"No one of Spanish descent would dishonor the memory of the bold explorer Coronado by masquerading as one of his men in order to commit crimes."

Longarm wasn't so sure about that. Greed made men do many things worse than dishonoring the memory of an explorer.

Ramon had reached the ranch house and disappeared inside. Now, suddenly, Longarm saw him come running out of the adobe dwelling. Ramon yanked the old Dragoon out of its holster and fired a shot into the air. The dull boom of the report rolled over the flat landscape.

Rosa leaned forward anxiously in the saddle and exclaimed, "Something is wrong!" She touched her spurs to her horse's flanks and sent the animal leaping forward.

Longarm was right behind her, thinking that of course something else had gone wrong. Hell, it had been almost half an hour since the *last* fracas.

Chapter 8

Ramon ducked back into the house as Longarm and Rosa galloped toward the hacienda. Despite the young woman's head start, Longarm caught up to her and passed her. His Colt was already in his hand as he reined to a stop in front of the open door and threw himself out of the saddle.

The ranch house wasn't fancy. It was a squarish building with thick adobe walls, a flat roof, an arched doorway, and rifle slits instead of windows. Likely when it was built, the Comanches under Chief Quanah Parker had still posed a threat, and the house had been constructed with an eye toward defense.

But the thick walls also kept the air inside pleasantly cool, even in hot weather, and that coolness washed over Longarm as he strode through the door into a living room.

He saw right away that there was no immediate threat. Ramon knelt next to a long, heavy divan where an old man lay stretched out. Blood left a bright trail on the man's leathery face. It had seeped down from a gash on his skull, next to where the thinning gray hair started.

Longarm saw the old-timer's chest rising and falling, so he knew the man wasn't dead. Ramon looked over his shoulder at Longarm and asked, "Where is Rosa? Alejandro is hurt!"

"I'm right here," answered Rosa as she hurried into the room behind Longarm. "What happened?"

Ramon shook his head. "I do not know. When I rode in I found Alejandro lying over by the corrals, unconscious. I brought him in here to make him more comfortable, then went back out to fire a shot, so you would know something was wrong."

The light in the room was dim, but enough illumination came through the open door and the rifle slits so that Longarm could see fairly well as he bent over the divan and studied the old man's wound. "Looks like somebody beat him with a pistol," he said. "He'll probably be all right if his skull's not cracked."

"Get a wet cloth, Ramon," Rosa briskly ordered her brother. "I will bring a bottle of wine from the kitchen. If we can get Alejandro to drink a little, it may bring him around."

Longarm figured a good stiff jolt of whiskey might be better for that, but he didn't say anything. They probably didn't have a jug of forty-rod around here. Instead he left Rosa and Ramon to tend to the unconscious old-timer and went back outside to have a look around.

Ramon had said he found Alejandro by the corrals. It was no trouble for Longarm to follow the marks made by the old man's boot heels as Ramon dragged him to the house. They led him to the place near the corrals where Alejandro had been knocked out. Longarm saw several dark spots on the ground where blood had spattered.

He saw, as well, a confused muddle of footprints. Several men had milled around here, all of them wearing boots. He followed the prints along the pole fence to the big barn. It occurred to Longarm that there were no horses in any of the corrals that flanked the barn on three sides. The barn doors stood wide open, and when he stepped inside and looked around, he saw that all the stalls were empty.

Longarm didn't know how many mounts Rosa and Ramon had in their string, but it looked like all of their horses were gone except for the one Rosa was riding. Of course, they had the horses that had belonged to the two dead bushwhackers. Longarm figured that under the circumstances, the Hernandez siblings had a better claim to those animals than anyone else. Still, it would be difficult for them to work their herd with only three horses on the ranch.

When he went back into the house, he found Alejandro conscious and sitting up on the divan, sipping from a glass of wine as he used his other hand to hold a wet cloth to his injured head. Rosa sat beside him with a worried expression on her face while Ramon paced back and forth looking mad.

"Let me guess," said Longarm. "Alejandro here was just telling you how some fellas came along and ran off all your horses."

"And when he tried to stop them, they attacked him," said Rosa. "They tried to kill him!"

The old-timer shook his head, wincing as the movement must have made it hurt worse. "No, señorita. If those gringos had wanted me dead, it would have been a simple matter for them to shoot me or kick me to death once they knocked me out."

Ramon turned sharply toward him. "Perhaps they saw us coming and fled like the cowards they are!"

"It wouldn't have taken but a second to pull a trigger," Longarm pointed out. "No, I reckon Alejandro's right. They didn't want to kill him. They didn't mind roughing him up a mite and stealing your horses, though. That was their way of sending you a message."

"Get off this range," Rosa said tautly. "That is what they were telling us."

Longarm nodded. "I reckon that's probably right."

"Barfield!" spat Ramon. "Did you get a good look at them, Alejandro? They were Box B riders, were they not?"

The old man winced again. "I . . . I do not know. They wore bandannas over their faces, and their hats were pulled down. I could not see them that well. And gringos . . ." Alejandro shrugged. "Most gringos look alike to me. I am sorry, *patron*."

Rosa patted his shoulder. "Do not worry. You tried to stop them. That was all you could do."

Ramòn swung toward the doorway. "I am riding to the Box B," he announced. "It is time we settled this with Barfield."

Longarm saw the look of desperate fear on Rosa's face, and he moved to put himself between Ramon and the door. "Hold on a minute, old son," he said. "I don't know if Barfield's to blame for your problems or not, but I guarantee you that if you ride in there full of piss and vinegar like this, there'll be trouble. Gun trouble, more than likely."

"Then what would you have us do? Sit back and allow a bunch of damned gringos to force us from our land? Again?"

"Best to eat the apple one bite at a time," Longarm told him. "I'm headed for the Box B anyway. Why not let me go down there and poke around some? If I find your horses on Barfield's spread, that'd be some proof you could take to the sheriff." He held up a hand to forestall Ramon's protest. "I know, you and your sister don't think much of Thurston. Neither do I. But even a sorry lawman like him would have to act if you put the proof right in front of him."

Rosa put in, "It sounds like a good idea, Ramon. Señor Parker is offering to help us, and I believe we would be foolish to turn him down."

"Señor Parker," repeated Ramon, scorn in his voice. "You would put your trust in a gringo you have known for little more than an hour? I thought you had more sense than that, Rosalinda." His lip curled in an angry sneer. "Perhaps you find this man handsome, so now you think with your heart instead of your head."

Rosa stood up from the divan and took a quick step toward her brother. Her hand flashed up and cracked across Ramon's cheek in a sharp slap. The movement was almost too fast for the eye to follow. With an indrawn breath, he stepped back, seeming more surprised than hurt by the blow.

"You will not speak to me in such fashion," she snapped. "I want only what is best for us and for this ranch. You know that, Ramon."

He touched his fingertips to his cheek, which glowed red where she had slapped him. With a surly glare, he said, "I beg your pardon, *hermana*." It was clear the apology wasn't overly sincere.

"You forget that Señor Parker risked his own life to rescue you from those gunmen not long ago," said Rosa. "It is true we have known him only a short time, but I . . ." She looked at Longarm. "I do trust him."

"And I'll do my best not to let you down, ma'am," he told her.

It bothered him a bit that he had agreed to go to work for Charley Barfield, and now he was heading for the Box B to spy on the man and his riders. Of course, it wasn't like the riding job he had taken with Barfield was the real thing. Longarm had always intended to use the job to find out the truth about what was going on here in the Panhandle. If Barfield really was trying to take over the Eagle Ranch by unlawful means, it was part of Longarm's job to put a stop to it.

There was the matter, too, of the suspicions Rosa and Ramon held about the Bloody Spaniard being tied in with

Barfield. That didn't seem possible, on the face of it, but Longarm had learned over the years not to disregard any possibility until he had absolutely proven it to be wrong.

So all in all, he didn't feel too bad about offering to help the Hernandez siblings. That went right along with the goals he already had.

He said, "I'll see if I can pick up the tracks of those stolen horses. If Barfield is to blame for running them off, I don't expect he'd take them straight to the Box B, but you never know."

"And if you find the horses, you will tell the sheriff?" asked Rosa.

Longarm nodded. "That's the plan." He didn't add that he might change that plan, if circumstances warranted. In a situation as murky as this one, it was difficult to know what to do until the time came to act. Even then, sometimes a fella couldn't be sure of the best course of action.

Since old Alejandro seemed to be all right other than an aching head, Longarm figured there was no need to fetch a sawbones from Tascosa. He said as much, then bid farewell to the three of them. Ramon was still in a bad mood and just grunted, but Rosa said, "*Vaya con Dios, señor.*"

Longarm mounted up and circled the ranch, looking for tracks left by the stolen horses. He found them headed south, toward the Box B, but within a mile the trail split into a dozen or more branches as the thieves broke up the herd and dispersed it every which way. Longarm didn't know who the fellas were, but they weren't stupid, he was sure of that. He continued riding south, knowing that it would be pointless to try to track the horses any farther.

His encounter with the Hernandez siblings had cost him more than an hour's time, but he wasn't worried about that. Instead, as he rode he thought about everything he had seen and heard during the past eighteen or so hours. It had been an eventful period. Unfortunately, the musing didn't bring him any closer to figuring out answers to the questions that needed answering.

He was still deep in thought when something caught his attention. He reined in, eyes narrowing as he stared at the strange sight ahead of him.

A man knelt on the ground, hands clasped in front of him as if in prayer, facing away from Longarm. As Longarm watched, the man suddenly leaned forward and started pawing at the dirt. Clods of earth flew in the air as he dug. Longarm's frown deepened as several minutes went by and the man continued to dig, paying no attention to anything around him. Longarm slowly walked his horse closer.

Abruptly, the man let out a yell. He came to his feet and thrust his hands in the air above his head as he began to dance a jig step that carried him around in circles. Whatever he was holding glittered in the sun.

He had gone around a couple of times in his dance when he saw Longarm and came to a sudden stop. Longarm reined in about ten feet from him. The man stared at him through rimless spectacles. He was bareheaded, his gray hair askew. The lack of a hat might explain his unusual behavior. The Texas sun beating down had caused more than one man to go loco.

Longarm recognized the man now. His name was Chapman, and he had been in the Deuces the night before with Sheriff Thurston. According to Charley Barfield, Chapman was a professor of some sort. Judging by how he'd been carrying on, thought Longarm, his title must be Professor of Foolishness.

Slowly, Chapman lowered his arms. "You must think I'm mad," he said without preamble.

"Looked more like you've had a touch of the sun," said Longarm. "Are you all right?"

Chapman laughed. "All right?" His spectacles slipped down on his nose. He pushed them up. "I'm more than all right. Look!" He held up the shiny thing in his other hand.

It was the rowel off a spur, Longarm realized. Bigger and with sharper points than the usual rowel on a cowboy's spur, it had a Spanish look to it. It was crusted with dirt, too, from being buried in the ground. Chapman had brushed some of the dirt off of it, uncovering the silver underneath and accounting for the reflections it gave off.

"This is one more bit of proof that I'm on the right track," exclaimed Chapman. His lean face was animated and excited. "This must have come from one of Coronado's men! Perhaps from Coronado himself!"

Longarm began to understand. "You're looking for artifacts," he said.

Chapman frowned slightly. "Of course," he said in the tone of an adult addressing a particularly slow-witted child. "That's what I do. I look for artifacts to prove that my theory about Coronado's journey through this area is correct."

"Folks have known for a long time that ol' Coronado passed through these parts when he was looking for the Seven Cities of Gold," Longarm pointed out.

"Yes, yes. But I'm tracing his exact path, which no one has ever done before. I've followed it all the way from below the Mexican border, across Arizona and New Mexico and now into Texas." Chapman brandished the rowel. "At each stage of the journey I have discovered artifacts such as these to prove that I'm correct."

"How you know that came from one of Coronado's conquistadors?" asked Longarm, gesturing at the rowel in Chapman's hand. "It's been over three hundred years, and there were other Spanish explorers who followed Coronado. Jose Mares and Pedro Vial came through these parts on separate expeditions a little less than a hundred years ago."

Chapman's eyes widened a little in surprise. "You

know of Mares and Vial? A simple, unlettered cowhand such as yourself?"

Longarm let the insult implicit in Chapman's words roll off his back. With a grin, he said, "Oh, I pick up a few interesting facts here and there, in the bunkhouses and the saloons and the dance halls." As a matter of fact, he was a frequent visitor to the Denver Public Library, especially during the last ten days of the month when his wages tended to run a little low and he had to make do with cheaper entertainment. He enjoyed flirting with one of the gals who clerked there, too.

"Who are you, anyway?" asked Chapman. "You look a bit familiar. Have we met before?"

"Nope, but you might've seen me in Tascosa last night at the Deuces. I was there with Charley Barfield when you came in with Sheriff Thurston. My name's Custis Parker."

Chapman grunted with ill grace. "Perhaps I did see you. I'm Dr. Andrew Chapman."

"You and the sheriff friends, are you?"

"Hardly. Acquaintances, at the very best. But he's a jovial sort and insists on buying me a drink every time he sees me in town. Personally, I think his conviviality is but an excuse for him to imbibe himself."

"Could be," allowed Longarm. "He strikes me as a fella who's pretty fond of the tonsil varnish, if you know what I mean."

He wasn't sure Chapman knew or not, but the professor didn't press the point. Instead, he said, "I had better be getting back to town so I can catalog this find."

Longarm looked around the empty prairie. "That's something else I was wondering about. Where's your horse?"

"Oh, I don't have one. Well, actually I do. I have two horses. I use them to pull my wagon. But they're back in Tascosa, at the livery stable."

"Then how'd you get all the way out here?"

"I walked, of course. I have to pay close attention to the ground, and I can see it better when I'm on foot."

"You *walked*?" said Longarm. "Clear out here, all the way from Tascosa?"

"Certainly. Coronado's men walked hundreds of miles during their expedition. I at least have a wagon to carry my equipment and baggage from town to town. But I do most of my searching for artifacts on foot."

Longarm shook his head. "You'll get heat stroke if you're not careful."

"Nonsense. I've tramped across the Gobi Desert in Mongolia. Conditions were much worse there than they are here."

Longarm knew only vaguely where those places were. Maybe Chapman was right. Maybe it *was* hotter and drier there. But that didn't make the idea of tramping around the Panhandle any smarter.

"Well, you be careful," he told the professor. "I've got to be riding."

"You're headed south. Are you on your way to the Box B?"

"As a matter of fact, I am." Longarm paused. "That mean anything to you?"

Chapman shook his head. "No, not at all. But you should be careful of Barfield. His men have tried to kill me more than once, you know."

Chapter 9

That bald-faced statement made Longarm stare. After a moment, he said, "What?"

"Barfield's men have tried to kill me several times," said Chapman, again adopting that patient, patronizing tone.

"How do you know that?"

"I've heard the bullets go past my head, and on occasion, I've seen them strike the ground near me. Since there doesn't seem to be anything else out here in this wasteland at which one could shoot, it is therefore a logical conclusion that the gunmen were shooting at me."

Longarm reined in the impatience he felt. "So somebody's tried to bushwhack you," he said. "How do you know it was Barfield's men?"

"I believe we're on his ranch. Who else could it be except his riders?"

"You mean you haven't actually seen the hombres who shot at you?"

"No, I simply deduced their identities."

Longarm scraped a thumbnail along his jawline. "But it could've been just about anybody, as far as you know for sure?"

"If you want to be stubbornly insistent about it, then, yes, I suppose you're right. I don't know for a fact that men from the Box B are responsible for the attempts on my life." Chapman fluttered a hand. "You go right ahead and ride in there, and when they shoot *you*, perhaps you'll see that I was correct."

"I don't reckon they'll give me a bullet welcome," drawled Longarm. "You see, they're expecting me. I'm going to work for Barfield."

Chapman's lips thinned and his face hardened. "Very well. I see now the sort of man I'm dealing with. Good day, sir." He turned his back and started striding away, still clutching the ancient Spanish rowel.

Longarm tried a shot in the dark. "Maybe it was the Bloody Spaniard who tried to plug you."

Chapman stopped short and jerked around to face him again. "What? What did you say?"

"Maybe it was the Bloody Spaniard who took those potshots at you," repeated Longarm. "Maybe since he's the ghost of one of Coronado's men, he don't much like you coming along and disturbing the things him and his compadres left behind."

The professor's lip curled. "You're insane! The so-called Bloody Spaniard doesn't exist. He's just a figment of the overheated imaginations of a bunch of fools and bumpkins!"

"Then I reckon I'm one of them bumpkins," said Longarm, "because I've seen the son of a bitch with my own eyes."

Chapman looked more interested now. "You've actually seen him?"

"Yep," Longarm said with a nod. "Not far from here, in fact. He wore armor like one of Coronado's conquistadors, and it glowed in the dark."

"No." Chapman's mouth got that stubborn set to it

again. "No, I don't believe it. There is no such thing as a ghost."

"That's what I thought. But I sure ain't come up with a better explanation for what I saw."

That was shading the truth considerably, thought Longarm. He did have a better explanation for the Bloody Spaniard: Somebody was putting on that old armor and running around the Panhandle for reasons of his own, reasons that Longarm hadn't figured out yet. But he would. Sooner or later, he would find out the truth.

"Believe whatever you wish to," said Chapman. "As for myself, I won't indulge in such foolishness."

"Suit yourself." As the professor started to turn away again, Longarm added, "One more thing. Did you tell Sheriff Thurston about somebody shooting at you?"

"Of course."

"Did he try to find out who it was?"

Chapman snorted scornfully. "Certainly not. To conduct a proper investigation of the matter would require a great deal more energy than the good sheriff appears capable of mustering."

At least that was one thing Longarm and Chapman agreed on.

Longarm sat there on his horse as Chapman stalked away across the plains, heading northeast toward Tascosa. As the stiff-backed figure dwindled in the distance, Longarm shook his head and turned his horse toward the Box B once more. He glanced at the sun, which was almost directly overhead. This trip out to Barfield's ranch was taking him a lot longer than he had expected.

And he had a lot more to think about now, too. The bushwhacking of Ramon Hernandez, the theft of the Hernandez horses and the attack on Alejandro Carranza, the attempts on the life of Professor Chapman . . . these were all things to add to the ledger when he toted up the score of banditry and lawlessness here in the Panhandle.

For a change, nothing else violent or unusual happened as Longarm rode on to the Box B. A short time later he came within sight of the ranch headquarters. The main house sat on the bank of a creek and had a couple of cottonwood trees shading it, the first real trees Longarm had seen in a while. The house was made of lumber, too, instead of adobe. The planks must have been freighted in from New Mexico. A hundred yards away, also near the creek, sat a long adobe bunkhouse. A couple of barns, several corrals, a cook shack with a tin stovepipe protruding from the roof, and a smokehouse completed the layout. It was a good-looking place, nothing fancy, but plenty solid.

Longarm had seen quite a few cattle bearing the Box B brand already as he rode across Barfield's range. More cows milled around a couple of the corrals. In another corral, a cowboy was working with a half-wild horse, swaying easily in the saddle as the broomtail pitched around. A couple of men sat on the top rail of the corral fence, watching idly. They turned to look at Longarm as he rode up. He recognized them from the night before. One of the men half-lifted a hand in greeting.

"Howdy, Parker. I think the boss expected you out here earlier this mornin'."

"I got delayed," said Longarm. "Is Charley up to the house?"

"Naw, he's gone out to check on some boys we got brandin' a bunch of mavericks. Ought to be back soon, though. Go on up there and set on the porch if you want. I reckon it'll be all right."

Longarm nodded. "Much obliged." He had started to turn his horse toward the house, when a whoop from the other cowboy made him stop. He looked around to see the bronc-buster sailing through the air to land with a crash in the dirt of the corral.

The cowboy rolled over, pushed himself onto hands and

knees, and shook his head dazedly. He came to his feet and started cursing the horse that had just thrown him.

"Took you by surprise, didn't he?" Longarm asked with a grin.

The bronc-buster stopped the stream of profanity in mid-cuss and looked around. "What'd you say, mister?"

Longarm nodded toward the horse. "I said he fooled you. Made you think you had him licked, and then all of a sudden he put his heart in it again. I've seen horses do that before. They're trickier than we sometimes give 'em credit for."

The cowboy picked up his hat and slapped it angrily against his leg. "You reckon you could do any better?" he challenged.

"My horse-breaking days are behind me," said Longarm, though a part of him was tempted to pick up the gauntlet. "You're doing fine. Just remember, no matter how smart the horse is, you're still smarter."

"I wouldn't bet a hat on that," cracked the other man on the fence. He and his companion grinned broadly.

Longarm just smiled, shook his head, and turned toward the house. None of these cowboys struck him as the sort to be rustlers and cold-blooded killers. He had seen some pretty bad men, though, who could be friendly and charming enough to beat the band . . . when they wanted to be.

He had been sitting in a wicker chair on the porch, long legs extended in front of him and crossed at the ankle, for about twenty minutes when Charley Barfield rode up. Several men were with him, including Arch Kellman. Kellman glared at Longarm and headed for the bunkhouse without a word.

Without being too obvious about it, Longarm studied the men who were with Barfield. He had gotten only a fleeting look at the gents who had lurked in that mesquite thicket to ambush Ramon Hernandez. He was relatively sure, though, that none of these riders had been among the ambushers.

"Well, you made it," said Barfield as he swung down from the saddle and looped his mount's reins over the hitchrack in front of the ranch house. "Expected you sooner."

"Sorry. I got held up."

Barfield frowned. "You don't mean that literally, do you?"

"Nope."

"Around here, these days, a fella never knows." The rancher came up the steps onto the porch. "Come on inside, and I'll write your name in the book. Dinner ought to be on the table soon."

The other cowboys who weren't out on the range drifted into the house and took places around a long dining table. An elderly cook with a bushy beard brought pots and platters of food from the cook shack, and the men dug in with gusto. Ranch work was hungry work.

"Thanks, Rosebud," one of the men said to the cook.

"Rosebud?" repeated Longarm from his seat halfway along the table.

The old-timer turned a belligerent glower toward him. "That's my name," he declared. "You want to make somethin' of it?"

Longarm held up both hands, palms out in surrender. "No, sir. It's a fine name."

"Damned right it is. You gimme any lip, I'll bounce one o' these here biscuits off your noggin."

One of the men put in, "And them biscuits are hard enough to do some serious damage to a fella's skull." That brought a round of laughter from the others and a slew of muttered curses from Rosebud.

All in all, it was a typical ranch meal, with only a little joking around, because the men concentrated on their food. Longarm enjoyed it and felt the camaraderie around the table. He hated to think that these boys might be a bunch of highbinders and owlhoots. But that wouldn't stop him from arresting them—or whatever else he had to do—when the time came.

Kellman hadn't come in to eat, Longarm noted. He supposed the man didn't care for his company. If that were the case, the feeling was mutual.

When the meal was over, it was time to get back to work. "Come on," said Barfield, motioning to Longarm. "Get yourself a fresh horse from the remuda, and we'll take a *pasear* around the place. That's the first thing a new man ought to do, familiarize himself with the spread where he'll be workin'."

Longarm nodded in agreement. Looking around was exactly what he had in mind.

Catching and saddling a fresh mount from the remuda gave him a chance to have a look at the other horses. He was still searching for the ones that had been ridden by the bushwhackers that morning. He saw a couple of horses that looked as if they had recently been ridden fairly hard. That wasn't proof, though, merely an indication that it was possible the gunmen had come from the Box B.

Longarm and Barfield rode out, heading still farther south. "Most of our best graze is down this way," said Barfield, "but we've got stock all over the range."

"What about your neighbors?" asked Longarm.

Barfield shot him a glance. "What about them?"

"I was just wondering how far the Box B runs in each direction."

"Oh." The suspicion vanished from Barfield's eyes. "I understand now. The ranch runs west to the New Mexico border, north to the Red River, and south to the head-waters of the White River. Over east it runs up to the edge of the LS Ranch and George Littlefield's LIT spread."

"Who are your neighbors the other directions?"

"Well, the XIT, which is owned by some fellas up in Chicago, sort of curves around us on both north and south."

Barfield hadn't mentioned the Eagle Ranch. Longarm was trying to think of a way to bring up Rosa and Ramon Hernandez when Barfield did it himself, continuing, "Oh, yeah, and there's a little piece of ground to the north bein' squatted on by a couple of Mexes. They're sort of sittin' there between me and the XIT."

"That so?" prodded Longarm.

"Yeah. I've talked to the manager up at the XIT about 'em. Seems the syndicate in Chicago figured on buyin' that piece of property when the old boy who owned it decided to pull out, but those Mexicans beat them to it. I asked why the syndicate didn't try to buy them out, and the manager said those Chicago fellas figure the ranch will fail sooner or later and the Mexes will abandon it. Then the syndicate can get the range for back taxes."

"You could, too," Longarm pointed out.

Barfield rubbed his jaw, which was beginning to bristle with beard stubble. "Yeah, I've thought of that. I don't really need it. It's pretty sorry range. But I don't like havin' a couple of thievin' Mexes squattin' there on the edge of my place, neither."

Longarm was well aware of the hostility most Texans felt toward folks from Mexico. It went back to a little mission on the banks of the San Antonio River called the Alamo, and another settlement known as Goliad . . . But Rosa and Ramon were from New Mexico and were American citizens. He might have pointed that out to Barfield, except for the fact that doing so would reveal he knew more about the Hernandezes that he was supposed to.

It occurred to him as well that since the owners of the vast XIT Ranch had their eyes on the Hernandez spread, Barfield might want to get his hands on the ranch so that he could turn around and sell it to the syndicate. When it came to a motive for Charley Barfield to want to run off Rosa and Ramon, the cattleman had more than one.

For the next several hours, Longarm and Barfield rode over the Box B range, heading south and then swinging back to the east and north in a broad circle. Barfield complained about the rustling that was going on in the area, and when Longarm mentioned the fact that the wideloopers hadn't struck the Box B, Barfield said glumly, "You mean they ain't hit us yet. It's only a matter of time."

They talked about the Bloody Spaniard, too, but Barfield didn't reveal anything that Longarm didn't already know. There had been no sign of the ghostly figure the night before when Barfield and his men headed back to the ranch from Tascosa.

The sun had slid a considerable distance down the western sky when Longarm and Barfield headed back to the ranch headquarters. "You've been on the payroll since dinner," Barfield commented, "but don't expect tomorrow to be so easy. I got cows spread out hell-west and crosswise all over this range. It takes a lot of graze for each cow, since there's not that much grass. So they tend to wander a far piece. You'll be ridin' the line from can to can't."

Longarm nodded and said, "I been there before. Do you partner up your hands?"

"Generally, yeah. Things can happen. A rattler can spook a horse and get a man throwed. A fella who was set afoot and hurt out here likely wouldn't make it if there was nobody around to help him."

"Probably be a good idea not to put me with Kellman, then. I don't think he cottons to me much."

Barfield laughed. "You can say that again! I reckon he'd be gunnin' for you if he didn't know I'd skin his hide for him if he did. He'll be a long time gettin' over that horse you shot out from under him. He ain't the forgivin' sort."

"Colt man, ain't he?" asked Longarm, a deliberately hard edge to his voice.

"He's got a rep as a gun thrower, sure enough. Most folks think that's why I hired him. But it ain't. He's a good hand, even if he is a mite surly most of the time. And if trouble does come to the Box B, he'll be a good man to have on my side."

"Drifted into this part of the country just about the same time as all the rustling and robberies started, didn't he?" Longarm's words were couched in a tone of idle speculation.

They had the desired result, though. "Yeah, I guess," Barfield said with a frown. "What're you gettin' at, Parker? You think Arch has something to do with—"

Longarm didn't have to answer the question Barfield was about to ask, because at that moment, the sharp, flat crack of a rifle split the late afternoon air.

Chapter 10

"What the hell!" exclaimed Barfield as he twisted in the saddle toward the sound of the shot. The report had come from somewhere off to the right, not too far away.

Hard on the heels of the rifle shot came the banging of pistols. Somebody was in trouble over there. Longarm and Barfield wheeled their horses and put the animals into a gallop.

They rode hard over the gently undulating prairie. Longarm couldn't see anything in front of them, even though the gunfire continued. He wasn't surprised when he and Barfield came to one of the dry arroyos that criss-crossed the Panhandle. The wash was about twenty feet wide and half that deep. Barfield sent his mount down the sloping bank, leaning back in the saddle as the horse's hooves slid on the sandy soil.

Longarm followed the cattleman. The bed of the arroyo was softer, so they couldn't ride as fast, but they hurried as much as they could. The shots were coming less frequently now, and as Longarm and Barfield approached, they died away completely. An ominous silence hung over the arroyo.

As Longarm rounded a bend, he spotted a couple of

horses up ahead. They were riderless, their reins dangling. Nearby, two dark shapes lay motionless on the sand.

"Damn it!" grated Barfield. "That looks like some o' my boys!"

He and Longarm reined in and quickly swung down from their saddles. Barfield ran to the closer of the two bodies lying on the sandy bed of the dry wash. Longarm was right behind him. Barfield knelt next to the man and grabbed his shoulder, rolled him over onto his back. The front of the cowboy's shirt was soaked with blood, and a dark spot on the ground marked where the sand had already sucked up more of the life-giving fluid. The young cowhand's eyes stared sightlessly at the fading light in the sky.

"Damn it," Barfield said again. "It's Tobe, and he's dead."

Longarm dropped to a knee beside the other man. "This one's still alive," he said as he found a pulse in the man's neck. Carefully, Longarm rolled him onto his back. This man's shirt was bloody, too. He'd been hit high on the chest. The rattling sounds he made as he breathed told Longarm he'd been drilled through the lungs. Longarm didn't figure he had more than a few minutes left.

"Get one of the canteens!" he snapped, forgetting for the moment that he was giving orders to the man who was supposed to be his boss. Barfield ignored that and hurried to do as Longarm said. He brought a canteen over and handed it to Longarm, who uncorked it and dribbled a little water into the mouth of the wounded man.

The young cowboy twitched and coughed, and pain-filled eyes opened. He blinked up at Longarm and gasped, "What . . . what . . ."

"Rest easy, old son," Longarm told him in a calm, steady voice.

"I . . . I'm shot!"

"Yeah, you are. Did you see who did it?"

The cowboy's gaze flicked past Longarm's shoulder. "Ch-Charley? Is that you?"

Barfield leaned over Longarm and said, "Yeah. Who done this, Jerry? Tell us if you can."

The cowboy gasped, trying to fill his lungs with air even though they didn't work right anymore. "Tobe and me . . . we saw some fellas . . . drivin' Box B cows . . . into the wash. We tried to follow 'em . . . Reckon they saw us . . . laid for us . . . We . . . we fought 'em, Charley . . . We done what . . . we could . . ."

"I know you did, son," Barfield said gently. "Did you see anybody you knew? Did you recognize the rustlers?"

Jerry's tongue came out of his mouth, rasped over dry lips. "They wore bandannas . . . like masks . . ."

The same bunch that had stolen the horses from the Eagle Ranch, thought Longarm, although logically he knew that didn't have to be the case. Anybody could pull a bandanna up over the lower half of his face.

The cowboy looked at Longarm again. "Am . . . am I gonna die?" His voice was weaker as he had to struggle even harder for the breath to form the words.

"I reckon so, old son. I'm sorry."

"My ma . . . Get word to my ma . . . down in Blanco County . . ."

"Don't you worry. We'll take care of it," Barfield assured him.

"And get . . . get the sons o' bitches who . . . who . . ."

Breath wheezed out of him, and he was gone. Barfield straightened, cursing bitterly. "We'll do it, Jerry," he said, though the young cowboy could no longer hear him. "We'll get the sons o' bitches, just like you said." He wiped the back of his hand across his mouth and added softly, raggedly, "Bet a hat on it."

Longarm got to his feet. "Why don't I take a look on down the wash?" he suggested. He was still giving orders, but in a more subtle fashion now.

"Yeah, go ahead. But be careful. Some o' those skunks could still be lurkin' around."

Longarm didn't think that was likely. Once the rustlers had disposed of the two cowboys following them, they would have taken off for the tall and uncut, driving the stolen cattle before them.

"I'll load these two boys on their horses so we can take 'em back to the house," continued Barfield. "Don't go too far, Parker. I don't want to lose you the first day you go to work for me."

Longarm swung up into the saddle and gave Barfield a curt nod. He rode along the arroyo, being especially watchful every time the gash in the earth made a bend.

It didn't take him long to find the tracks of cattle and horses. They led plainly along the sandy bed of the dry wash. The rustlers had driven off a small jag of cattle, maybe fifty head. Not a big raid, but a definite start. Now nobody on the Box B could say that the rustlers hadn't hit the ranch.

The rustlers had driven the stock up a shallow bank and out of the wash about half a mile beyond the spot where the two cowboys had died. Longarm reined in and looked to the northwest, where the tracks led. There was nothing in that direction except the New Mexico line. By the time he rode back to Box B headquarters and gathered some men to come with him after the stolen stock, the wide-loopers would likely have the cows across the border, where buyers who didn't gave a damn about brands would be waiting. Longarm shook his head. It looked like the rustlers had won this round.

And those two young cowboys, Jerry and Tobe, had lost.

Longarm caught up to Barfield, who was leading the two extra horses with their grisly burdens, before the cattleman got back to the ranch house. He reported what he had found. Barfield grated a curse and then said, "With a bunch that small, they can push across the line fast enough we wouldn't stand a chance of catchin' up to them."

Longarm nodded. "That's the way I figured it, too."

"Still, it bothers the almighty hell out of me not to even try goin' after the bastards."

"I reckon we'll get another chance at them. Now that they've had a taste, they'll come back for a full meal."

Barfield rubbed his jaw. "Maybe so. This bunch ain't been shy, that's for damned sure. Ever since they popped up, they been actin' like they can do anything they want around here without worryin' about anybody from the law doin' anything about it."

"Sheriff Thurston's not much good, is he?"

"Clyde Thurston might've been a good man once," said Barfield with a grimace. "But he got fat and lazy."

"What about the Rangers?"

"Some of the businessmen in town and the other ranchers got together and wrote a letter to Ranger headquarters in Austin, askin' for help. Ain't nothin' come of it, though. I guess the Rangers have all got better things to do right now."

Longarm knew that wasn't the case, but he couldn't say anything, not without revealing his own identity. Instead he said, "Looks like it's up to us, then."

"Yeah. I'm gonna have the men ridin' longer hours than ever, keepin' an eye out for rustlers."

"Might be a good idea to set up regular patrols with more men in each group," suggested Longarm.

"Yeah. That's just what I'm goin' to do."

They came within sight of the ranch house. Someone must have spotted them leading the horses, because several men rode out hurriedly to meet them. Loud, angry curses filled the air as the Box B cowboys saw the bodies of Jerry and Tobe.

It was a somber bunch at supper that night. Nobody

spoke much, not even to hooraw the old cook Rosebud. Death had a way of doing that. Barfield picked several men to dig graves. The two murdered punchers would be laid to rest the next morning.

When the meal was finished, most of the men withdrew to the bunkhouse. Longarm lingered and said to Barfield, "Somebody ought to ride into Tascosa and tell the sheriff what happened, whether Thurston cares or not."

Barfield nodded slowly. "I reckon you're right."

"I can do it, if you want. I know my way around well enough now I won't have any trouble finding my way there and back in the dark."

"You sure?"

"Yeah, I don't mind." Longarm hadn't said anything to Barfield about the raid on the Hernandez ranch, and he had promised Rosa and Ramon that the law would be notified. He could take care of that chore at the same time.

He had seen most of Barfield's range today and hadn't found any sign of the stolen horses. It looked more than ever like Rosa and Ramon were wrong in their suspicions about Barfield. In fact, it seemed to Longarm that the Eagle Ranch and the Box B were pretty much in the same boat as targets of the gang that was running roughshod over the Panhandle. They ought to be working together, rather than suspecting each other of villainy.

It wasn't easy to get people to see something like that. Casting blame was a lot easier.

Longarm saddled another horse and rode out. As he passed the barn, he saw a flicker of movement inside the open door. He thought he caught a glimpse of Arch Kellman glaring out at him, but he couldn't be sure. Kellman had been at supper, but he'd sat at the far end of the long table and hadn't said a word to anybody as far as Longarm knew.

The skin on the back of Longarm's neck prickled. He was riding off into the dark, and Kellman might know that. The situation was tailor-made for trouble if Kellman followed him.

Longarm wasn't going to back out on the chore because of that. He kept right on, riding steadily and easily over the plains toward Tascosa.

It occurred to him that he would be passing the place where the Bloody Spaniard had appeared the night before. He'd had a good look at the area that morning, and he hadn't seen anything to indicate why the glowing phantom had chosen that spot to manifest itself. The ghost had been just passing through on its way somewhere else, Longarm decided.

Of course, he still didn't believe the hombre was a ghost, but somehow it was easier to think of him that way. Where had the Spaniard been headed when Barfield and the Box B riders had spotted him and taken off after him?

Longarm turned his head to peer off into the darkness. The Hernandez ranch was in that direction, and beyond it lay the vast reaches of the XIT and the wilds of New Mexico Territory. Had the Spaniard been going to see Rosa and Ramon? They had claimed to know nothing about him—unless, of course, he was tied in with Barfield, as they had been quick to suggest. But they hated Barfield, or at least Ramon did, and they had been mighty eager to try to cast suspicion on him . . .

Longarm grimaced and shook his head. The questions and the possible answers went round and round in his head, and he wasn't any closer to figuring out what was going on than he had been twenty-four hours earlier when he first saw the ghostly glowing figure.

Just like he was seeing it now, he realized with a shock that went through him like a physical blow. Up ahead and off to the left about two hundred yards, a man-shaped glow moved steadily through the darkness. Longarm reined in sharply and stared at the thing.

Wherever the Bloody Spaniard had been going the night before, he was headed there again.

Chapter 11

He would never have a better opportunity to find out what was going on around here, thought Longarm. For the second night in a row, the mysterious Bloody Spaniard was putting in an appearance. Things appeared to be heating up in the Panhandle. Longarm had gotten to these parts just in time.

And now he was going to follow that glowing figure. The moon hadn't risen yet, and though the starlight was fairly bright, Longarm didn't think the Spaniard would spot him if he kept a good distance between them. With his quarry shining like that, Longarm wouldn't have to be very close to stay on the trail.

Longarm loosened his Winchester in the saddle boot, then put his horse into an easy trot, turning the mount's head so that he was traveling northwestward. The ghost didn't seem to be in any hurry. Longarm was careful not to move in too close. He didn't want the Spaniard to hear the hoofbeats of his horse, but he figured as long as he couldn't hear the Spaniard's horse, the armored figure couldn't hear him, either.

On the other hand, maybe the apparition was riding a ghost horse, and its hooves didn't make any sound.

Under the sweeping mustaches, Longarm's mouth twitched in a half-grin, half-grimace as that thought went through his mind. He reckoned he was getting carried away with all this ghost business. The Spaniard was flesh and blood, and Longarm wasn't going to believe otherwise unless and until it was proven to him.

He kept an eye out for lights that marked the location of the Hernandez ranch. With every minute that passed, it appeared more and more likely that the Spaniard was on his way to see Rosa and Ramon. For all he knew, he thought suddenly, the Spaniard might *be* Ramon Hernandez! Ramon carried a powerful grudge against all gringos. What better, more fitting way to strike back at the objects of his hate than to rob from them and kill them while wearing the ancient armor of his ancestors? If that ancestor had been one of Coronado's men, the armor might have been handed down from generation to generation in the Hernandez family. The more Longarm thought about the theory, the more sense it made.

The only problem was that despite being hot-blooded and full of rash, youthful anger, Ramon Hernandez hadn't struck him as an owlhoot and a murderer.

Maybe he would know before much longer, thought Longarm. They couldn't be very far from the Hernandez spread now.

With no warning, a gun suddenly blasted from somewhere close by. Longarm heard the wind-rip of the bullet only inches from his ear. He bit back a curse as he twisted in the saddle, searching for the source of the shot. He knew he had only himself to blame for being bushwhacked like this. He had gotten so caught up in following the Spaniard and trying to figure out what was going on that he had forgotten about the threat of Arch Kellman.

A second shot rang out, and this time Longarm spotted the Colt flame blooming in the darkness off to his left. His own revolver was already in his hand. He triggered twice at the muzzle flash and then bent forward in the saddle as he kicked his mount into a gallop. The horse responded instantly, lunging ahead. Longarm heard the roar of another shot and the whine of a bullet, but this one wasn't as close. He returned the fire as he tried to circle around whoever had ambushed him and turn the tables on the son of a bitch.

Disaster struck again with no warning. One of the horse's front legs went out from under him. The animal fell heavily, throwing Longarm from the saddle. He kicked his feet free from the stirrups just in time. As he went sailing through the air, he thought fleetingly that the horse must have stepped in a prairie dog hole or something like that. Not that the cause really mattered. What was important was that Longarm was now at even more of a disadvantage.

He hit the ground hard, knocking the breath out of his body. Though stunned, his brain kept working well enough to send him rolling over and over on the sandy ground. Somehow he had hung on to the Colt, though he knew there was only one bullet left in the cylinder. If he used it, he would have to make the shot a damned good one.

Coming to a stop on his belly, he raised his head and looked around. His vision was blurred because the fall had gotten some grit in his eyes. He saw something coming toward him, something that glowed like a lantern . . .

It was the Spaniard, thought Longarm, as he heaved himself up on his knees, the damned Bloody Spaniard. The thing, whatever it was, charged toward him, the hoof-beats of the phantom's horse thundering in the night. Longarm blinked and pawed at his eyes with his free hand as he lifted the Colt in the other. Tears washed out the grit, and his sight cleared. The Spaniard was practically on top of him, the glowing figure looming up out of the night.

Longarm tipped up the revolver's barrel and fired, flame geysering from the muzzle of the Colt. He heard a loud *clang!* and an instant later, as he threw himself aside, the horse's shoulder struck him a glancing blow. The impact was hard enough to knock him spinning through the air.

For the second time in a matter of moments, Longarm crashed into the ground. This time his head hit something hard, and he felt the jolt all the way through his brain. Skyrockets went off behind his eyes. As their garish red glare faded, only blackness was left behind. Longarm felt consciousness slipping away from him and tried desperately to cling to it, knowing that the night was full of enemies and that if he passed out it was mighty likely he would never wake up.

The effort failed. Everything was gone, and he was lost, alone, drifting in a sea of nothingness.

Over his years as a lawman, Longarm had been knocked unconscious enough times to know that pain was a good thing. The agony in his head as he swam up out of the blackness meant that he was still alive.

He was no longer alone in the oblivion. He heard the tramping of feet, the shouting of voices. Orders were called in Spanish. Somehow time had rolled back, and he was with Coronado, marching across a trackless waste, the sun beating down with brutal heat, all in search of gold, elusive gold.

Time slid away again, and he was in a land that had never known the touch of European feet, a land where the horse was unknown and no one lived except small, primitive bands of hunters. Then the earth shook and mountains rose and fell, and a great flood covered the land as the very continents themselves were made and remade and eternity rolled back and back until all was nothingness again, a nothingness that waited for a divine spark, a fusion of what had been and what was and what would never be . . .

That must have been one hell of a wallop, he thought as he blinked his eyes open and then squinted them to shut out some of the light that struck painfully against them. It had knocked him plumb addlepated for a spell, but he was himself again now.

A groan came from his lips, and something soft and blessedly cool draped itself across his forehead. "Please, Señor Parker," said a sweet voice. "You must rest."

Longarm blinked a couple of times and looked up into the lovely face of Rosalinda Hernandez.

She seemed worried, and after a moment he figured out that was probably because she thought he was badly hurt. He could have told her that it would take more than a clout on his iron-hard noggin to do any real damage . . . but the cool cloth on his forehead felt so good, and the way she stroked his cheek with her fingertips was mighty nice. It was easier and much more pleasant just to lie here, wherever here was, and enjoy being cared for and fussed over. Besides, his head *did* hurt like a son of a bitch. He sighed and closed his eyes, allowed a half-sleep to steal over him.

Even in that state, he heard Rosa murmuring soft words of comfort.

After a time, a little imp in the back of Longarm's brain started acting up. The pesky varmint reminded him that just before he'd blacked out, he had been ambushed by someone unknown while following the Bloody Spaniard. And the Spaniard himself had nearly ridden him down and trampled him. Longarm recalled firing a shot. Again, he heard the ringing report of a bullet against metal, and the memory made him realize something important. He had shot the Spaniard! That hurried shot had struck the ghostly figure's armor. But had it penetrated, or had the armor done its job and sent the slug glancing off?

He wondered as well how he had wound up in Rosa's hands. He was mighty glad that he had, but it was still a curious situation.

Like it or not, he told himself, he was going to have to open his eyes again and start asking some questions.

"Rosa . . . ?" he whispered as he forced his eyelids up.

She was still there, right beside him. "*Sí*, Señor Parker?"

"H-How . . . how did I get here? And where am I?" His voice was a little stronger by the time he finished asking the two questions.

"You are at our ranch, of course." Lamplight shone on her face, and she blushed prettily in its glow. "In my bed, as a matter of fact. As for how you got here, Ramon and I heard the shots and rode out to see what was wrong. We found you lying on the ground, unconscious."

More of Longarm's wits had returned to him by now. As he shifted slightly, he felt smooth, cool sheets against bare skin. He realized he was naked and wondered if Rosa was the one who'd stripped his clothes off him.

She answered that question by saying, "At first we thought you had been shot, but after we brought you back here we made sure there were no bullet wounds on your body."

So she had at least been there when somebody took his clothes off, he thought. Or maybe she wasn't speaking literally. He didn't know.

"I found a bump on your head," continued Rosa. "What they call a goose egg, no?"

"Yeah, a goose egg is about right," said Longarm. "And a mighty big goose, at that."

Rosa smiled. "*Sí. El grande* goose."

Longarm swallowed, suddenly aware that his mouth was dry and that he was very thirsty. That could wait, though. "Did . . . did you see anybody else?"

Rosa shook her head. "No, only you. We found your

horse, though." Her expression grew grim. "The poor beast had fallen and broken its leg. Ramon put it out of its misery."

Longarm closed his eyes for a second and sighed. This assignment had been damned hard on horseflesh so far.

He looked at Rosa again. "But nobody else was around?"

"No," she said. "Did someone attack you, Señor Parker?"

"You could say that," muttered Longarm. He took a chance. "It was the Bloody Spaniard."

Rosa's eyes widened. "The Spaniard? You are sure?"

"His horse nearly trampled me. I got a shot off at him, too. I think I hit him."

If she knew anything about that, she did a good job of hiding it. Her expression was a mixture of disbelief and surprise. But she said, "If the Spaniard was there, he was gone by the time Ramon and I found you."

Unless the Spaniard had been Ramon Hernandez all along and Ramon had brought Longarm back here to Eagle, thought Longarm. But the Spaniard had acted like he wanted him dead. If that were the case, why hadn't the ghostly figure finished him off while he lay there unconscious?

Maybe if that had been Ramon in the armor, he hadn't realized who Longarm was until after he'd nearly trampled him. Maybe the Spaniard hadn't really meant him any harm and had just been trying to see what all the shooting was about.

Too many questions, too many possible answers. Longarm's head hurt already, and trying to puzzle out this mess only made it ache worse.

Still, there was something else he wanted to know. "Where's Ramon now?"

"Riding around the ranch, watching for trouble. He and

Alejandro plan to remain alert all night. Ramon thinks the rustlers may strike again."

That was a possibility, thought Longarm. The appearance of the Bloody Spaniard always presaged trouble of some sort. That was assuming, of course, that Ramon wasn't the Spaniard himself.

So he and Rosa were alone in the ranch house, Longarm mused. That could have been an intriguing situation, if he hadn't been recovering from being knocked cold earlier tonight. As it was, he didn't figure he was in any shape for amorous shenanigans. Not that Rosa had given him any indication she was interested in such things. But he figured that it was a good sign he could even think about it.

He hoped the day never came when he couldn't.

A great weariness came over him after that, and he let himself doze off again. He knew the thing he needed most right now was rest. His iron constitution, hardened by the vigorous life he had led for so many years, would recover rapidly.

When he came awake again, it was not nearly as unpleasant as it had been when he regained consciousness the first time. In fact, it was downright nice to lie there on clean sheets and feel the soft warmth of bare female flesh pressed against him all up and down his body . . .

Longarm's eyes snapped open. He'd been correct about what was happening. He lay on his left side, and a naked Rosa Hernandez was cuddled against him spoon-fashion, her back to him. The thick waves of her raven hair were spread out on the pillow next to him, and the clean, invigorating scents of her hair and skin filled his nostrils. Faint light came into the room through some curtains hung over the single window, and when Longarm raised his head slightly, he could see Rosa's profile. The hour was early, around dawn, and the glow of the new day shone on her smoothly curving cheek as she slept. She was achingly beautiful, thought Longarm.

She was also having a definite effect on him. His manhood had hardened into a long, thick bar of male flesh that poked against the cheeks of her rump. She shifted a little in her sleep, and the wiggling of her backside changed things around so that his shaft slipped right between her thighs. Longarm felt the damp heat of her femininity pressed against the upper side of his organ.

It would have been damned easy to angle his hips a little and thrust forward so that his shaft would go right between those tempting folds of female flesh. He had never taken advantage of a gal while she was asleep . . . unless, of course, he knew her well enough to be sure she would enjoy being woken up that way. That wasn't the case here. In fact, he felt a surge of unaccustomed embarrassment, both for himself and for Rosa.

But, he reminded himself, she was the one who had climbed into bed with him this way. They wouldn't be lying here together if it weren't for her. It *was* her bed, he recalled, but still . . .

He realized that his hand rested in a familiar fashion on her bare hip. He was about to remove it when she shifted again. Her arm moved under the sheet. She put her hand over his, and to his surprise, she clasped it and moved his fingers over her skin. It was almost as if she were caressing herself but using his hand to do so. She slid his hand over the flat plane of her belly, up to her rib cage and then onto her right breast. She squeezed and so did he, feeling the warm globe of flesh fill his palm. The nipple hardened under his touch, poking out and forming an erect little bud of pebbled flesh. He stroked it with a fingertip.

Lord, she was wet! he thought as her hips moved slowly, sensuously, back and forth. Her eyes were still closed and he thought she was still asleep, but clearly, she was aroused. Those feelings of need and desire had welled up inside her, even as she slumbered. He couldn't stop his own hips from moving in response to her. His shaft slid along her opening, spreading the wetness. He clenched his teeth as he struggled to rein in the almost overpowering impulse to penetrate her. A fella could only fight against nature for so long a time, and then he would have to give in.

The only solution was to get the hell out of this bed and away from her while he still had that choice. He started to move while he still could, pulling away from her . . .

Her thighs clamped together hard, trapping his throbbing shaft between them. "Ah, *Dios mio!*" she exclaimed. "If you do not make love to me right now, señor, I think I shall die!"

Chapter 12

Longarm caught his breath. He leaned over, brushed his lips against her cheek in a kiss. "You're awake?" he murmured.

"*Sí.*" Rosa panted a little through open lips. "I know it is shameless, but I must have you. Please, Señor Parker . . . Custis . . . please take me now."

Longarm wasn't in the habit of making beautiful women beg. He drew back just enough to aim himself properly and then obliged her with a surge of his hips that imbedded most of the length of his shaft inside her.

She let out a low, throaty cry as he sheathed himself within her. Longarm hoped that Ramon and Alejandro were still out riding the range and not in the next room. Rosa seemed to think it was safe for them to be doing what they were doing. She thrust her hips back against him so that he was buried even deeper in her.

Longarm slid his other arm underneath her and brought his hand around to cup her left breast. He kneaded and caressed both of her breasts as he began a slow, steady, strong surging with his hips. Burying his face in her hair, he searched until he found the back of her neck. His lips sucked lightly on her skin.

He continued driving in and out of her. She reached back with her right hand and caught at his hip, the fingers digging into his flesh as she urged him on. She panted and murmured words of endearment, intermingled with what sounded like prayers. Longarm plucked at her nipples, kissed her shoulders. The pace of their lovemaking remained slow but deeply powerful.

The passion within them built up gradually but inexorably. Longarm felt his need for culmination boiling and rising inside him. His embrace tightened around Rosa. She would have been writhing by now if not for his strength. As it was, she twisted her head around on her neck and reached up so that their lips met in a heated, urgent, searching kiss. Her mouth broke apart from his with a gasp as she began to shake from the sensations cascading through her.

Longarm surged forward one final time and froze with his manhood at its point of deepest penetration. He shuddered as he began to empty his seed into her in a series of throbbing, searing, white-hot explosions. Their juices mingled, bubbled, overflowed, drenching both of them. Longarm's jaw tightened as he bit back the shout of pure pleasure that threatened to well up from his throat. Rosa couldn't control her reaction. Her cry of ecstasy filled the room.

Both of them were covered with a fine sheen of sweat as they slumped against each other, muscles limp in the aftermath of the climaxes that had shaken them. His arms gradually loosened around her, and his softening organ slipped out of her.

She turned over to face him, staying within the circle of his embrace as she did so. Their lips found each other again. Now that the urgency was gone, they were able to lie there and luxuriate in a long, slow, wet kiss. Their lips opened and their tongues met, gliding and swooping around each other as they explored. Rosa drew up a knee and threw her leg over Longarm's hip, resting it there companionably. He stroked her flank and felt her flesh quiver slightly under his touch.

"*Gracias,* Custis," she whispered when they finally broke the kiss. "It has been so long . . . since I have truly felt like a woman."

"I was mighty glad to oblige," Longarm told her. "It was my pleasure."

She laughed. "It was *our* pleasure."

Longarm couldn't argue with that.

Although he hated to break the mood, after several minutes of their lying there petting and caressing each other, he said, "About your brother . . ."

Rosa nodded. "*Sí,* Ramon and Alejandro will be back soon. I must get dressed and prepare breakfast for them, and for you as well. Are you hungry?"

Longarm became aware that he was indeed ravenously hungry. "I could eat," he allowed. "A pot of coffee would be nice, too."

"I will see to it." She started to get up, then paused to reach out and lightly touch his head. "Your goose egg is much smaller this morning."

Longarm checked the lump on his skull for himself. "Yeah, it's more like a banty hen's egg now," he said with a grin.

Rosa smiled at him and got out of bed. Longarm's eyes feasted on the nude, tawny length of her as she stretched languorously in the dawn light. Then she pulled on a long skirt and a scoop-necked white blouse and left the room.

Longarm laced his hands together behind his head as he lay there staring up at the adobe ceiling of the bedroom. He felt wonderfully refreshed, and his thoughts turned naturally to the case. A few minutes later, the tantalizing aromas of coffee boiling and bacon cooking threatened to distract him, but he forced his mind back on track. Unfortunately, he didn't come up with any new answers. He still didn't know who the Bloody Spaniard was or exactly how the ghostly figure tied in with the wave of lawlessness. His hunch that the Spaniard was really the boss of the outlaw gang was as strong as ever. Could a young man like Ramon have managed such a thing? Could he have gathered together a bunch of cut-throats and owlhoots? It seemed unlikely, and even less likely that he could control such a gang if he managed to assemble one.

But a cold-blooded gun thrower like Arch Kellman on the other hand . . .

Longarm was intrigued by that possibility. Kellman had turned up in the Panhandle at just about the same time as the Spaniard. The problem with that idea was that Kellman had been with Barfield and the other Box B cowboys a couple of nights earlier, when Longarm had first seen them chasing the phantom rider in golden armor.

But what was to say there couldn't be *two* men wearing that armor at different times? Longarm frowned. If Kellman was tied in with the outlaws, if indeed he was really the Bloody Spaniard, what better way to throw off suspicion than to have a bunch of witnesses see the Spaniard while Kellman was with them?

Longarm gave a little shake of his head as Rosa called, "Breakfast is ready!" He swung his legs out of bed and stood up to get dressed. For a second or two he felt dizzy, probably an aftereffect of the wallop on the head, but then his balance returned to him and he was able to pull his clothes on.

The food and coffee smelled even better when he stepped into the other room. Rosa had the meal on the heavy table in the center of the room. She and Longarm sat down to eat. She had heated up tortillas, scrambled some eggs, and crumbled bacon into the eggs before rolling them in the tortillas. There were beans as well, and plenty of hot sauce that set Longarm's mouth on fire. He washed down the food with several cups of strong coffee, and by the time he was finished, he felt almost completely recovered. A night's sleep, a bout of passionate lovemaking, and a good meal never failed to work wonders.

The sound of hoofbeats came from outside. Rosa stood up, a smile on her face. "That must be Ramon and Alejandro," she said. She went to the door to greet them.

Ramon looked tired and worried when he came into the room, followed by the elderly vaquero called Alejandro. He threw a none-too-friendly glance at the tall, rangy gringo sitting at the table, then tossed his dusty sombrero onto a hook on the wall next to the door.

"Did you see any rustlers, Ramon?" asked Rosa.

He shook his head. "No, but another twenty head of our cattle are gone."

Rosa lifted a hand to her mouth in surprise. "No!"

"*Sí*. They vanished from our southern range." Ramon glared at Longarm again. "This man you think so highly of rides with thieves, Rosalinda!"

Longarm placed his hands flat on the table and kept his temper under control. "If you're talking about Charley Barfield and the boys from the Box B, I think you're wrong," he said. "Fact of the matter is, they lost fifty head to the rustlers yesterday and had two men killed in the process. In broad daylight, too."

"You did not tell me about that, Custis," said Rosa. Longarm saw the glance her brother gave her when she used his first name. She went on, "If the rustlers are stealing from the Box B now—"

"Bah!" Ramon cut in. "It means nothing! Barfield pretends to steal from himself because he knows that to do otherwise would be too suspicious."

Longarm stood up and shook his head. "You're wrong, old son. I was there when one of those Box B cowboys died, and so was Barfield. He didn't have anything to do with it."

He didn't say anything about the theory starting to drift around in the back of his mind that Arch Kellman might be tied up with the outlaw gang somehow, might even be the ramrod of the wild bunch that had moved into the Panhandle.

Ramon gave him a cold stare. "I brought you into this house because my sister insisted that we must. But I do not trust you, señor, and if you are recovered enough from your injury to travel, I think it would be best if you left our ranch."

Rosa bristled. "Ramon, how dare you—"

Again he interrupted her. "Rosa, you are my older sister and I must respect you, but you are only a woman. The time has come for me to give the orders on this ranch."

Longarm saw the anger flare in Rosa's eyes. She could be as hot-blooded and short-tempered as her brother when the mood was on her, as it was now. She stepped toward Ramon, her hand lifting to slap him again, as she had done the day before. This time, however, his own hand shot out and grasped her wrist before she could strike the blow. The two of them stood there like that, locked together, seemingly frozen in place as they glared at each other with only a few inches between their faces.

"*Patron*," said Alejandro. "*Patron*, please . . ."

"Better let go of her, old son," said Longarm in a quiet tone that was fraught with menace.

Abruptly, Ramon shoved Rosa's hand down. "Never strike me again," he grated.

"Never presume to think you can give me orders!" she flared back at him.

They would have to work this out between them, thought Longarm, but in the meantime, at least he could remove one of the things they were fighting over, namely him. He moved away from the table, saying, "I need to get on into Tascosa. That's where I was headed last night when I ran into that ambush." He didn't mention the

Bloody Spaniard. Rosa could tell her brother about that if she wanted to.

Ramon looked at him with an unfriendly expression that was half-grin, half-snarl. "It will be a long walk, gringo."

"I was hoping I could borrow a horse."

"We have only three horses now, remember? And two of them are exhausted from being ridden all night. As soon as I eat, I intend to take the fresh horse back out on the range to watch for those *chingado* rustlers."

Longarm frowned. He and Ramon might not get along too well, but the youngster had a point. Longarm couldn't very well take the only fresh horse on the place.

As if sent from above, the clip-clop of hooves sounded outside the ranch house. Alejandro turned to the door and looked out. Over his shoulder, he said, "*Ai de mi!* It is that loco old gringo."

Longarm heard the creaking of wagon wheels as he followed Rosa and Ramon to the door. The three of them, along with Alejandro, stepped outside to see Professor Andrew Chapman pulling a wagon with a two-horse hitch to a halt near the water trough. He wore a hat today, and he lifted a hand to touch the brim as he nodded politely to Rosa. "Good morning, madam," he said. "And good morning to you gentlemen as well. I was wondering if I might be allowed to water my team?"

Ramon might have refused the request simply because of the color of Chapman's skin, but before he could speak Rosa stepped forward quickly and waved a hand toward the water trough. "Go ahead, señor. There is plenty of water."

Chapman nodded to her again. "Thank you, madam." He flapped the reins. The horses stepped over to the trough and lowered their heads to drink.

While they were doing that, the professor climbed down from the wagon seat and stretched. No one had asked him to light down, so doing so was a minor breach of frontier etiquette, but Longarm figured that being an Easterner, Chapman probably didn't know that.

Rosa was polite. She said, "There is coffee and food inside the house. Will you join us, señor?"

Chapman looked a little distracted. "Eh? Oh, no, but thank you. I appreciate the generous offer. Indeed. Appreciate it very much. But I've already eaten this morning." He turned his gaze toward Longarm. "Ah, my mysterious friend. I see no one shot you when you rode up to the Box B yesterday."

"Nope," agreed Longarm, not mentioning the other trouble he had run into since his last encounter with Chapman. "Are you by any chance heading into Tascosa, Professor?"

"As a matter of fact, I am. I spent last night on the prairie, communing with the stars."

"Reckon I could hitch a ride with you?" Longarm knew that if he could get to Tascosa, he could rent another horse at the livery stable. The thought made him grin faintly. Ol' Henry up there in Denver would pitch a hissy fit when he saw the expense vouchers for this case. Henry was a regular Cerberus when it came to guarding the budget for Billy Vail's office.

"To Tascosa, you mean?" asked Chapman with a frown.

Longarm suppressed a flicker of irritation. It appeared the professor couldn't keep his mind on a subject from one moment to the next. "That's right," he said patiently. "I've been set afoot."

"Certainly, certainly. I'll be glad of the company."

"I'm much obliged." Longarm turned to Rosa. "When you brought me here last night, did you fetch my saddle and gear?"

"Sí. Alejandro took care of them," she replied.

"Your things are in the barn, señor," said Alejandro. "I

will get them for you." The old-timer turned away.

Longarm lifted a hand to stop him. "No, that's all right, I can get them. *Gracias,* though." To Chapman, he added, "I'll be right back, Professor."

Ramon had listened to the conversation with arms folded across his chest and a petulant glare on his face. Now, as Longarm went into the barn, the young man drifted after him. Longarm wasn't sure if Ramon wanted something or was just keeping an eye on him because he suspected all gringos of being untrustworthy.

Ramon wanted something. In a low voice that couldn't be overheard by those outside, he said, "You are not welcome on this ranch, señor. You would be wise not to return to it."

Longarm found his saddle sitting on a sawhorse. The Winchester was propped against it. He picked up the rifle and said, "You aim to shoot me on sight or something, Ramon?"

"Perhaps."

"You seem to have forgotten how your sister and I pulled you out of that bushwhack trap yesterday."

"Do not insult me. I forget nothing." Ramon's lip curled in a sneer. "But a debt owed to a gringo is less than nothing. Besides, you have been handsomely repaid, have you not? We took you in last night when you were injured, cared for you, gave you shelter. You even slept in my sister's bed."

He really would be on the prod if he knew what else had gone on in that bed, thought Longarm, who had sense enough not to mention that. And Ramon was right about the debt being repaid. He said as much.

"So we're square, old son," Longarm went on. "Just remember, I don't much cotton to being threatened."

"It is not a threat. It is a promise."

Longarm hefted the saddle, returned Ramon's cold stare for a second, and then turned to walk out of the barn. As

115

he did so, a spot in the middle of his back itched. The feeling was all too familiar.

It came from knowing that Ramon would have liked to put a slug right through him . . .

Chapter 13

Longarm carried his saddle and rifle toward the professor's wagon. The vehicle had an arched canvas cover over the bed, and as Longarm approached the back of it, he saw that flaps of canvas were also drawn over the opening above the tailgate, closing off the inside of the wagon from view. He would have shoved the flaps aside and put his saddle inside the wagon, but at that moment Chapman hurried over to him.

"Let me take that for you," said Chapman as he tried to snatch the saddle out of Longarm's hands. Longarm hung on to it. The professor went on, "I'll put it in the wagon. You can say your farewells to these fine people."

Longarm frowned. He heard an edge of desperation in Chapman's voice. Was there something in the back of the wagon the professor didn't want him to see?

A possible answer to that question burst on Longarm's brain. He didn't want to force the issue at the moment, however, so he wiped any trace of suspicion off his face and out of his voice as he nodded and said, "Why, sure, Professor. Thanks." He let go of the saddle, allowing Chapman to take it from him.

He turned away from the wagon, playing along. He

stuck out his hand to Alejandro, who took it tentatively, with a worried glance at Ramon. The young man just looked away, pointedly ignoring what was going on.

"*Muchas gracias,*" Longarm told the former major-domo. "Thanks for everything, Alejandro."

"Thank the señorita," murmured the old man.

"I intend to," Longarm assured him. He turned to Rosa. "Problem is, there ain't no way I can thank you enough, ma'am, for everything you've done for me."

"Take care of yourself, Señor Parker," she said. "That will be thanks enough."

She put out her hand. Longarm took it, squeezed it. Though the contact between them was apparently innocent, he felt the spark leap as their hands touched. Neither of them would ever forget what had happened early that morning as the soft gray light of dawn crept into Rosa's room.

Longarm nodded to her, then turned and went to the wagon. He didn't waste time, energy, or breath trying to say goodbye to Ramon.

Professor Chapman had finished stowing away the saddle in the back of the wagon. The canvas flaps were pulled tightly shut again. He brushed his hands together, summoned up a not-too-convincing smile, and said, "Ready to go?"

"Ready, Professor," replied Longarm. He stepped up onto the driver's box with ease while Chapman climbed onto the seat more awkwardly.

Rosa waved as the wagon rolled away from the ranch house. Alejandro even ventured a slight lifting of one hand. Ramon, though, just stalked into the house, clearly glad to see the two gringos leaving.

"That young man doesn't seem overly fond of you, my friend," commented Chapman as he flapped the reins against the backs of his team.

"I reckon you could say that," Longarm agreed with a

grin. He swayed slightly on the wagon seat, rocking back and forth to the rhythm of the vehicle. The Winchester was propped between his knees, the barrel pointing at the sky.

Chapman handled the horses fairly well. That wasn't surprising. If he had followed the route he had mentioned the day before, from the starting point of Coronado's expedition down in Mexico, across Arizona and New Mexico and now into the Texas Panhandle, that meant he had driven hundreds of miles in the wagon. He ought to know how to handle it and the team by this point.

Of course, thought Longarm, Chapman might have been lying about all that. After all, the professor had something to hide there in the back of the wagon. That much had been obvious from his behavior. Now, Longarm asked himself, what could Chapman be hiding?

A suit of conquistador's armor, maybe?

Once the possibility had occurred to Longarm, back there at the Hernandez ranch, he began to go over everything that had happened. Chapman wandered around all over this part of the country, and folks seemed to think he was just a harmless eccentric. Nobody would suspect an addlepated professor of being the ramrod of a bunch of gun-tough killers and rustlers and thieves. Hell, he might not even be a real professor!

Longarm had a hunch that much of Chapman's story was true, though. If Chapman had been retracing Coronado's steps, he could have discovered the suit of armor somewhere along his journey. He might have even put it together from bits and pieces found at different places. But what had inspired him to go on the owlhoot? Longarm didn't know, didn't even know if he was barking up the right tree with his suspicions of Chapman.

But he knew he intended to get a look in the back of the wagon. That was for damned sure.

He wanted to do it without arousing Chapman's suspicions, though. The trip into Tascosa would take a while. Longarm decided that he could afford to bide his time.

Meanwhile, he would try to find out a little more about the professor, so that he could judge whether or not the man was telling the truth. "Whereabouts is it you teach?" he asked.

"Ah, Strickland University, in New England," replied Chapman. "It's a small school, quite exclusive."

Longarm had never heard of the place. He wondered if Chapman had just made up the name. It was possible Strickland was a real university, of course. Longarm supposed he hadn't heard of every single college and university in the country.

"I'm the head of the history department, currently on sabbatical," continued Chapman, evidently warming to his subject. "I've been meaning for years to carry out an exploration and recreation of Coronado's journey across the Southwest in search of the Seven Cities of Gold, and this year I was finally able to arrange things so that I can do so."

"Been a dream of yours for a long time, eh?"

"Lord, yes! What could be more fascinating?"

Longarm could think of quite a few things that were a lot more interesting than a bunch of Spanish soldiers tramping around and nearly dying of starvation and thirst. Some of those things in recent days involved Lady Arabella Winthrop and Señorita Rosalinda Hernandez. But he didn't figure Chapman was really looking for an answer to the question, so he kept his mouth shut and those sweet memories to himself.

"I saw that spur rowel you dug up," he went on. "I reckon you must've found a lot of things like that on your trip."

"Of course. The trail left by Coronado and his men was littered with artifacts. Of course, over the years many of them have already been picked up by scavengers and are now lost to history. But you'd be surprised at all the things I've found along the way."

Maybe not as surprised as you'd think, old son, mused Longarm. He reached into his pocket, slid out a cheroot, and found a lucifer in another pocket. When he had the cheroot lit, he blew a smoke ring that floated on the air for a moment before breaking apart in the light breeze.

"I never knew any professors before," he lied. "What sort of money does a fella make in your line of work?"

"Oh, it's not about the money," said Chapman, taking one hand off the reins to wave it in the air in a gesture of dismissal of the very idea. "The sheer joy of the knowledge itself is what motivates myself and most of my colleagues."

Longarm grinned. "It don't pay much, eh?"

"Not much," admitted Chapman. "I had to save for years to pay for this expedition. The university underwrote only part of the expense."

Longarm nodded slowly. Maybe that was the answer. Maybe Chapman was telling the truth about his quest for knowledge, but such things could be expensive. A fella might turn to outlawry to pay for something he really wanted to do . . .

Longarm thought back over everything he had learned so far about the Bloody Spaniard. As far as he could recall, the ghostly figure hadn't done much except ride around and be seen here and there. The professor was middle-aged, but he was leathery and wiry and probably plenty capable of riding a horse. If he was running the gang and providing his brainpower, he didn't have to be a good hand at brawling or shooting. Being smart might be enough.

Of course, Longarm reminded himself, there were those mysterious murders that had taken place about the same time the Spaniard was spotted lurking around Tascosa. A newspaperman, a sheriff's deputy, a store owner, and three drifters had all been victims of some unknown killer. Could Chapman have carried out those murders? One of the men had been beaten to death with a whip, Longarm recalled. As he glanced over at the professor, he supposed it was possible, even if not probable. It didn't take much strength to shoot or stab a man. That whipping, though . . . It gave Longarm a little pause. He wasn't sure he could accept the idea of Chapman beating a man to death.

Again, though, even if Chapman were involved with the outlaws, even if he wore the suit of glowing armor from time to time, that didn't mean he was the only one who ever wore it.

Chapman went on talking about Coronado and the academic disagreements—controversies would be too strong a word—over the exact route of the famous expedition. Longarm listened with only half an ear. Coronado had never found Cibola, Quivera, and the other fabled cities of gold, but somebody had found a good payoff here in the Texas Panhandle, somebody leading a vicious gang of murderers, wideloopers, and holdup artists.

And, Longarm realized to his frustration, he wasn't much closer to discovering who that mastermind was than he had been when he first rode into the Panhandle.

The rest of the journey to Tascosa passed without incident. Professor Chapman rattled on the whole way. He had said he would be glad for the company, and he had proven it. Likely he was just glad to have somebody to talk to after spending so much time alone out on the prairie, thought Longarm.

As the wagon rolled down the cattle town's main street, Longarm said, "You can drop me off at the livery stable. I've got to see about renting a horse."

"What happened to the one you were riding yesterday?" asked Chapman.

"Stepped in a hole and broke his leg," Longarm replied

shortly. He didn't say anything about how he'd been trading shots with a bushwhacker at the time, or about the phantom figure who had nearly ridden him down.

"That's a shame. I've heard it said that Texas is a wonderful place for men and dogs, but hell on women and horses."

Longarm shot a glance at the professor. He had heard that same saying many times, but he was surprised that Chapman was familiar with it. He supposed Chapman had been around the frontier long enough now to pick up quite a few things.

Chapman brought the wagon to a halt in front of the livery stable. Holding the Winchester in his left hand, Longarm put his right hand on the seat and vaulted quickly to the ground beside the vehicle. "I'll get my saddle," he said. He intended to be at the back of the wagon, pulling those canvas flaps aside, before Chapman could get there.

"Wait just a moment!" said Chapman. "I have your saddle right here." He reached behind him, through a similar set of flaps that hung over the front opening, and hauled Longarm's saddle into his lap. "I pushed it on up to the front when I put it in so it would be easier to retrieve when we got here."

Longarm tried not to frown at the slick way Chapman once again had thwarted his plans. Maybe there was nothing intentional about it; maybe Chapman had done what he said exactly for the reasons he'd said . . . but he couldn't have blocked Longarm any more neatly if he'd tried.

He reached up to take the saddle from Chapman. "Much obliged for the ride," he grunted.

"Not at all. It was my pleasure. Perhaps I'll see you around town again before I leave."

"Pulling back out, are you?"

"Yes, but not until later in the day. I need to replenish my supplies."

Longarm switched the rifle to his right hand and propped the saddle on his left shoulder. "Be seein' you, then." He turned and walked into the livery stable, trying not to reveal his disappointment at his failure to find out what Chapman had in the back of that wagon.

Longarm made arrangements with the liveryman to rent another mount and picked out a rangy buckskin from the horses in the corral behind the barn. He wouldn't need the buckskin right away, though, so he left his saddle and rifle there and walked back along the street.

He was looking for the sheriff's office, intent on finally carrying out the errand that had sent him to Tascosa from the Box B the night before, when he heard a female voice say, "Hello, Custis."

He looked over at the boardwalk and saw Lady Arabella Winthrop standing there. She wore a dark blue dress and a matching hat, and she carried a parasol in her hand to protect her skin from the harsh Texas sun.

"Mornin', ma'am. You look as pretty as a picture," said Longarm honestly.

"I didn't expect to see you again so soon," said Arabella. "I do hope there's no trouble out on Mr. Barfield's ranch."

"Well . . . a little." He didn't want to go into detail about the rustling and the killing of the two young cowhands, Tobe and Jerry. "As a matter of fact, I'm looking for the sheriff's office."

"It's right down there." Arabella pointed. "You won't find Sheriff Thurston there at this time of day, however. He's probably still asleep over at Maude's." She almost, but not quite, sniffed in contempt as she said the name.

"That another saloon?" asked Longarm.

"A house of ill repute." Arabella's tone was icy. "A large, yellow-painted house on the edge of town."

Longarm sucked on a tooth for a second as he thought about what to say. He had seen some of the girls in the Deuces making obvious arrangements with customers for carnal get-togethers later. It struck him as a mite hypocritical for Arabella to look down on a whorehouse and its proprietor. On the other hand, Arabella didn't allow the actual carrying-on at the Deuces, so maybe she was on slightly higher moral ground. Longarm didn't know, didn't really care. He had long since stopped trying to puzzle out all the intricacies of the mysterious mechanism known at the female brain.

"Fine and dandy," he said. "And thanks." He ticked a finger against the brim of his hat.

Arabella stopped him from turning away by asking, "Would you care to have lunch with me in a little while, Custis?"

"That sounds mighty nice. Thanks again." He could delay his return to Barfield's ranch for that long, he thought.

"In an hour, then. My room, upstairs at the Deuces." Her eyes sparkled. "You know where it is."

"Yes, ma'am, I sure do."

As Arabella went on her way, twirling the parasol, Longarm wondered if she had more in mind than just sharing a meal with him. It had been less than five hours since he'd made love to Rosa Hernandez, he thought. Sure looked like he was in demand today. But a lawman's work was seldom done, he told himself with a grin as he headed for Maude's place to find the sheriff.

Chapter 14

Longarm didn't have any trouble finding Maude's. It was the only house in Tascosa painted an ugly shade of mustard yellow. The front was made of rough-hewn planks; the rest of the house was the usual adobe. Longarm opened the door without knocking, stepped inside, and found himself confronted by a large, bald, sleepy-looking black man who moved with smooth quickness despite his seeming lassitude.

"New in town, boss?" asked the man, but somehow he made the "boss" sound not the least bit subservient.

Longarm put a cheroot in his mouth and clenched it unlit between his teeth. "You must be Maude," he said.

Anger flared for a second in the man's eyes, then was replaced by amusement. "You can call me Maude if you want. Might not answer, but you can call me that."

Longarm shifted the cheroot to the other corner of his mouth and said, "We could keep this up all day if we wanted to, old son, but I ain't interested in a pissin' contest. I'm looking for Sheriff Thurston."

"Maude" grinned. "Well, why didn't you say so? You don't aim to shoot him, do you?"

Longarm thought that he wouldn't waste a bullet on

such a slothful creature as Thurston, but he just shook his head and said, "Nope. Got some crimes to report."

The bald head moved slowly up and down in a nod. "Oh, well, then you come to the right place, boss. You go right ahead and wake up the sheriff. He's right down that hall, third door on the left. I'm sure he'll be powerful pleased to see you."

Longarm was torn between wanting to buy this fella a drink and wanting to punch him in the face. He settled for a cordial nod and moved on through a dingily furnished parlor that was deserted at this time of day.

As he started down the hall, a door on the right opened and a naked young woman stepped out. She was Chinese, with long, straight, shining black hair that reached most of the way down her back. Slender, with apple-sized breasts and smooth golden skin, she made no move to cover herself. Longarm couldn't help but notice that the usual triangle of hair at the base of her groin had been shaved off, leaving her femininity bare and slick as a whistle. She practically exuded exotic sensuality, and as she gave Longarm a smile, his teeth clenched a little harder on the unlit cheroot. He managed to nod politely to her, though, and his voice sounded normal to him as he said, "Mornin', ma'am."

Still smiling, she spoke to him in Chinese. He had no idea what she said, but he returned the smile and nodded again, then started past her toward the door of the room where Sheriff Thurston was supposed to be.

The woman stopped him by putting a hand on his groin and groping his organ through his trousers. Longarm took the cheroot out of his mouth and said, "Another time, Maude."

She laughed and let go of him. She ran one hand over her head as if she were bald and used the other hand to stroke the shaved area between her legs. She laughed again.

Feeling a mite bumfuzzled, Longarm went on to the third door on the left, leaving the young Chinese woman to wander off toward the parlor. A faint musky scent hung in the air. He recognized it as opium. Out here on the frontier, a fella just never knew what he was going to run into, even in a little trail town like Tascosa.

He knocked on the door but didn't wait for a response before opening it. With his right hand ready to draw the Colt if need be, his left grasped the knob and turned it. With a shove, he pushed the door back and stepped into the room.

Midday sunlight filled the room, barely blunted by gauzy curtains over the single window. The room was narrow, most of its floor space taken up by a bed with a sagging mattress. If the heavyset sheriff spent most of his nights here, that was probably the reason the mattress sagged, thought Longarm. Wearing a pair of dirty long johns, Thurston sat up, groaning and knuckling his eyes. The naked Mexican girl who lay beside him rolled over and went back to sleep.

"Do you know what time it is?" demanded Thurston in his high-pitched voice. "What the hell do you want?"

"I want to make an official report, Sheriff," said Longarm.

"Report? Report o' what?"

"Two murders, a fair amount of rustling, and some stolen horses."

Thurston ran blunt fingers through his tangled hair. "Oh, Lordy." The sheriff made shooing motions. "Go on over to the office and tell my deputy all about it. It's too damned early . . . I can't think—" Thurston grimaced. "Wait a minute. I ain't got no deputy no more. I remember now. Bastards all quit on me after what happened to poor ol' Fletch."

Fletch McAuliffe, Longarm recalled. That was the name of the deputy who had been one of the murder victims here in Tascosa. Why would the Spaniard target Mc-Auliffe and leave the sheriff and the other deputies alone?

Maybe McAuliffe had been the only one of the local lawmen whom the Spaniard regarded as a threat. It didn't seem likely that Thurston would ever catch the Spaniard or even discover his identity, and evidently the other deputies had all quit at the first sign of danger. Longarm frowned, sensing that he might be on to something.

In the meantime, though, he still had to get through this unpleasant bit of business. He hated to see somebody as sloppy and worthless as Thurston wearing a badge. That gave all star packers a bad name. Suppressing his irritation, he said, "Why don't you get up and get dressed, Sheriff, and we'll go over to your office and talk about it?"

"You tellin' me how to do my job, mister?"

Somebody sure as hell needs to, thought Longarm. But he said mildly, "Nope, just making a suggestion."

"All right. I'll be there in a few minutes." He turned to the girl who lay beside him and put his hand between her legs. Without looking at Longarm, he said, "You go on now, mister. I'll be there in a while."

Longarm's hands clenched into fists. He turned away, telling himself that he couldn't afford the time it would cost and the trouble it would cause if he beat the ever-lovin' daylights out of Thurston the way he wanted to.

There was no sign of the Chinese woman as he went out through the parlor, but the bald-headed black man was still there, sipping from a snifter of brandy. "I take it you found our illustrious enforcer of the law?"

"Yep. I'm obliged for the help, Maude." Longarm paused at the door. "I was just wondering . . . is there really a Maude?"

The black man tossed back the rest of the brandy and then licked his lips. "Is any of this real?" he asked. "Or is it all merely an illusion, the fever dream of a madman?"

Somebody was mad, all right, thought Longarm. He got the hell out of there, hoping that it wasn't catching.

He sat in a chair on the porch in front of the sheriff's office and lit the cheroot. He'd smoked it most of the way down by the time Thurston limped across the street. The sheriff wore a gray shirt that had once been white and a black cowhide vest. A dusty black Stetson was shoved to the back of his head.

"Go on inside," he said, waving a meaty hand at Longarm.

The office was dirty and cluttered, which came as no surprise considering its occupant. Longarm shoved aside a stack of papers on a broken-down divan, and as he sat down he was careful to avoid the wicked-looking springs poking through the upholstery.

Thurston went behind the desk and sank into a swivel chair. It creaked ominously under his weight. He dropped his hat on the blotter and sighed. "All right, mister," he said. "Make your report."

"Aren't you going to write it down?" asked Longarm.

"I got a good memory. Now get on with it. I got a hell of a hangover, and I need a little hair o' the dog."

Quickly, Longarm gave the sheriff the pertinent details about everything that had happened the previous day, from the bushwhacking of Ramon Hernandez to the killing of the two cowboys on the Box B. He stopped short of mentioning his encounter with the Spaniard on his way into town that night, however. He wasn't sure why he didn't say anything about it, but his instincts told him to hold back something. Though it seemed highly unlikely that the gang would consider Thurston any sort of threat, it was just possible that they might have paid him off to look the other way while they carried out their depredations. Longarm decided it would be best not to let Thurston in on any of his suspicions.

"Well, mister," said Thurston when Longarm was finished, "it sounds to me like you're the one to blame for all the trouble."

Longarm's eyebrows lifted in surprise. "What?"

"Hell, it's followin' you around, seems like. Ever'where you go, somebody starts shootin'."

"That ain't *my* fault!" protested Longarm.

"Maybe not, but things was rambunctious enough around here 'fore you showed up. Now hell's a-poppin' right and left. Why don't you do us all a favor and go back where you came from? Either that, or rattle your hocks and drift on to wherever you're goin'."

Now Longarm's eyes narrowed in anger. "Are you telling me to get out of town?"

"Damn right. You're a troublemaker. I'm a professional lawman, you know. I can recognize trouble when I see it."

Longarm suppressed the impulse to reach across the desk, grab Thurston's shirt, jerk him to his feet, and slap some sense into him. But that wouldn't put him any closer to rounding up the outlaw gang that was his reason for being here in the first place. Neither would it help to announce his true identity, strip the sheriff of his badge, and declare that from now on, he was in charge of the law around here. For one thing, it wouldn't really be legal to do so. A Texas Ranger could get away with such a thing, but not a deputy U.S. marshal who was on sort of shaky jurisdictional footing to start with.

"I'll get out of town, all right," he said curtly, "but I'm just going back out to the Box B. I reckon Charley Barfield will need all the hands he can get before this trouble is over."

"Maybe it's already over," said Thurston, a whining note entering his voice. "Maybe those damned owlhoots have looted enough around here and will ride on."

Longarm drew a deep breath, still struggling with his

temper. "You ever hear of Australia, Sheriff?"

Thurston looked confused. "It's one o' them foreign countries, ain't it? Clear around on t'other side of the world?"

"That's right. They got a bird there called the ostrich. Great big thing with long legs. But whenever there's trouble, the ostrich digs a hole in the sand real quick-like and sticks his head in it. He figures that if he can't see the trouble, the trouble can't see him."

"What's that got to do with anything?"

As if he hadn't heard the interruption, Longarm went on, "But the ostrich forgets about one mighty important thing . . . Its head may be in the sand, but its big ol' butt is still sticking up there, a damn good target for anything that wants to come along and bite it."

With that, Longarm stood up and stalked out of the office, leaving a confused-looking Sheriff Thurston behind the desk.

He stopped on the porch to light another cheroot and bring his anger and frustration under control. What he needed now was something to get the bad taste of the encounter with Thurston out of his mouth, so he headed for the Deuces and that lunch with Lady Arabella Winthrop.

He went up the rear stairs and down the hall to her room. When he knocked on the door, she called, "Come in."

He halfway expected to find her lounging nude on the bed, but instead she still wore the dark blue dress, though she had taken off the hat. She was so pretty he wasn't even too disappointed. She stood next to a table set with fine china and crystal glasses. A bottle of wine was on the table, along with several platters of food. Longarm saw roasted chicken, baked potatoes, some crisp greens, and corn on the cob, as well as a plate of biscuits that looked considerably softer than the ones Rosebud cooked up out at the Box B. After the good breakfast at the Hernandez ranch, he hadn't thought he'd be hungry again for a while, but at the sight of all the good food, his mouth began to water.

Arabella looked a mite mouthwatering, too, he thought. He took off his hat, hung it on a hook, and closed the door behind him. "Everything looks mighty good," he said.

"I pride myself on knowing how to satisfy a man's hungers," Arabella said with a smile.

"Yes, ma'am," said Longarm. "I expect you do."

Her smile widened as she picked up one of the glasses and poured wine into it. Longarm sat down as Arabella poured the wine and dished out the food. He dug in, eating hungrily and with enjoyment. As a rule, he wasn't that fond of wine, preferring Maryland rye or a good cold beer, but he had to admit that for washing down good vittles like this, it worked just fine.

"Did you find Sheriff Thurston?" asked Arabella.

Longarm nodded. "Yeah. I ain't sure I want to talk about it, though. At least not while I'm eating."

Arabella laughed. "Yes, I understand. Our good sheriff isn't the most appetizing individual in the world."

"You can say that again."

"But I won't, thank you. I prefer not to dwell on the unsavory. I *am* curious, though, about the trouble you mentioned out on the Box B. I'm fond of Charley Barfield. He's big and rough and can be crude at times, but I think he's a good man."

Longarm nodded. "So do I. I ain't so sure about at least one of the fellas he has working for him, though."

"Let me guess . . . Arch Kellman."

"That's right," Longarm said after taking a sip of the wine. He decided to take a chance, feeling an instinctive liking for Arabella that had little or nothing to do with her beauty and her enthusiasm in bed. It had to do with trust instead. He continued, "I'm wondering if Kellman might have something to do with all the problems that've been busting loose in these parts."

Arabella frowned. "Do you think that's possible?"

"He showed up about the time the trouble started," said Longarm with a shrug. "And he seems like the sort that wouldn't shy away from a little law-breaking."

"Yes, that's certainly true," she agreed. "Have you said anything about this to Charley?"

"Not yet. Thought I'd better mull it over a mite, first."

"Yes, that's a good idea. You're new around here, Custis. Charley might think that *you* were acting suspiciously if you started casting aspersions on one of his men."

"Yeah. I intend to keep poking around, though."

"Why? It's not really any of your business, is it?"

"I ride for the Box B," Longarm said flatly, giving the response that any self-respecting cowboy would have. Loyalty to the brand was one of the most important things in life to such men. "Besides," he went on, "I've got a personal grudge to settle with that hombre in the conquistador's armor. He nearly stampeded his horse right over me last night."

Arabella's dark eyes widened in surprise. "What?"

Longarm explained how he had run into the Spaniard on his way into Tascosa and then been ambushed as he was trying to catch up to the ghostly figure. "I reckon I put a dent in his armor with that slug," he concluded. "Chances are the Spaniard wants to find me just as much as I want to tangle with him again."

"You should be more careful," said Arabella, but then she shook her head. "I'm wasting my breath, aren't I? Being careful simply isn't in your nature."

"I don't always go rushing in where angels fear to tread." Longarm grinned. "Just part of the time."

"I'm not worried about angels," said Arabella. "I was thinking more of ghosts. As you said, ghosts in conquistador's armor . . ."

Chapter 15

The rest of the meal was very pleasant, but as it turned out, Arabella didn't have anything else in mind. When they had finished eating, she said, "That was very nice, Custis. You're a real gentleman, despite that rough-hewn exterior of yours."

"Thanks . . . I reckon," said Longarm with a wry smile.

"So I know that you'll excuse me now without any hard feelings. I have a great deal of paperwork to take care of. I do my own books, you know."

Longarm shook his head. "Nope, I didn't know that."

"Women aren't supposed to be very good with numbers, or so I've been told. Men tend to tell them not to worry their pretty little heads over such things. But I've always been a good hand at it, as they say here in cattle country."

Longarm lifted his rangy form from the chair and smiled at her. "Ma'am, if you want to go to cipherin', don't let me stop you."

Arabella toyed with her empty wineglass as she said, "You know, I sometimes get the feeling that you're not quite the unlettered frontiersman you pretend to be, Custis."

She was getting pretty close to the truth, he thought, especially the part about him being something other than what he was pretending to be. He picked up his hat and settled it on his head. "You're right, ma'am. I'm as deep as a well in the desert."

She laughed, just as he'd expected. "Go on with you. I'll see you later. Or are you riding back out to the Box B?"

"I expect I'd better. Charley and the boys thought I'd be back late last night. For that matter, so did I. They may be a mite worried about me."

"All right. I was hoping you might have dinner with me tonight, after I have this work taken care of and we'd have time to . . . relax. But I won't keep a man from his job."

That slight hesitation in her voice made the offer mighty tempting, thought Longarm. He had work of his own to do, though. "Another time," he said.

"Yes. I'll hold you to that."

With a sigh, Longarm left the room. Being discreet about it, he went down the rear stairs and turned into the alley leading to Tascosa's main street. He returned to the Deuces, this time through the front door. He intended to pause there just long enough to have a beer before he picked up his newly rented horse at the livery stable and headed for Charley Barfield's ranch.

When he went into the saloon, though, he saw that he wouldn't have to hurry. Barfield himself stood at the bar, along with several of his men. The big cattleman had a mug of beer in his hand. When he saw Longarm, he lifted it in greeting.

"There you are, Parker," said Barfield in his booming voice. "Damn it, man, when you didn't come back to the ranch last night, we all thought something had happened to you. Thought maybe that damned old Bloody Spaniard had gotten you."

138

Barfield was just a hair this side of being drunk, thought Longarm as he went over to join the rancher. He glanced at the other men. Arch Kellman was one of them.

"Hello, Charley. Sorry I didn't make it back when I said I would."

"I figured we'd better come lookin' for you. When we got into town, though, I saw the sheriff. He told me you'd been to see him and that you'd told him about Tobe and Jerry and the stock we lost." Barfield's eyes narrowed. "Said you told him about some horses bein' stole off the Hernandez place, too. How'd you know about that? You friends with those greasers or somethin'?"

A slightly hostile tone crept into Barfield's voice as he asked the questions. Longarm didn't want the rancher getting too suspicious of him, so he shrugged and said, "I just stopped by there to water my horse on the way out to your place yesterday morning. The girl happened to mention they'd been raided and lost some horses."

"You didn't say nothin' about that to me when I was tellin' you about those two and how they been a thorn in my side."

"Didn't see any point in bringing it up. It was pretty clear you don't like those folks."

"And their ranch is out of the way if you're ridin' from Tascosa out to the Box B," continued Barfield. "I don't like folks who throw in with my enemies."

Longarm felt a little flare of anger go through him. "Doesn't seem to me like the Hernandezes have a big enough ranch to qualify as anybody's enemies. They're just trying to get by as best they can."

"How do you know? You said you just stopped there to water your horse. Sounds to me like you know 'em pretty well." Barfield upended the mug and drained the rest of the beer from it. "I ain't sure I can trust you after all, Parker."

Kellman spoke up for the first time, a self-satisfied

smirk on his lean, dark face. "What the boss is saying, Parker, is that you're fired. You don't ride for the Box B anymore."

Barfield thumped his empty mug on the bar. "That's right." He started to dig in one of the pockets of his trousers. "I'll give you your time—"

"Keep your money," said Longarm, his voice curt. "I didn't earn any wages. You fed me a meal. That's enough to call it square." He shot a narrow-eyed glance at Kellman. "Reckon you got what you wanted, old son."

"I don't have my horse back," snapped Kellman. "Or your hide pinned to the wall." His right hand hovered near the walnut grips of the Colt holstered on his hip. "If you really want to square things, though, I'm ready any time you are."

It was damned tempting, thought Longarm. He was angry, and he wanted to settle the festering friction between him and Kellman. But killing the man wouldn't serve any real purpose, at least not at this point, and besides, Longarm knew better than to draw on a man when he was mad. Winning a gunfight took steady nerves and a cool, calm brain.

"I'll keep that in mind," he said to Kellman.

The gun thrower sneered. "You mean you're backin' down."

"I mean I'll settle things when I'm good and ready. And until then," added Longarm, "I'll keep an eye out behind me."

Kellman's saturnine features flushed with anger. Longarm had just pretty much called him a back-shooter, and everybody in the saloon knew it.

There was no telling what might have happened if the bulky figure of Sheriff Thurston had not pushed through the batwings just then. Thurston wasn't the sort to get involved and break up a fight that could prove potentially dangerous to him as well as the participants, but his arrival dispelled the tense mood. He paused just inside the door, his hands still resting on the batwings, and stood there for a moment, clearly contemplating whether or not he should back out of the saloon while he still had the chance. Then Professor Andrew Chapman stepped up behind him and said, "What's wrong, Sheriff? I thought we were going to have a drink."

"Uh . . . yeah," said Thurston. He swallowed and pushed on into the room. Conversation had died away during the confrontation between Longarm and Kellman, but now the noise in the place rose back to normal levels as Thurston limped over to a table and sat down with the professor.

Longarm said quietly to Barfield, "You're making a mistake, Charley." Then he turned away from the bar, pointedly ignoring Kellman, and started toward the door. He was angry with Kellman, frustrated with Barfield, and none too happy with himself for allowing this situation to develop. Without the job on the Box B, he was back where he had started, with no real excuse for hanging around Tascosa while he continued his investigation. He didn't really see what he could have done differently under the circumstances, but he was still peeved by these developments.

He paused on the way to the door, stopping beside the table where Thurston and Chapman sat. The sheriff had contributed to this problem with his big mouth, thought Longarm. Maybe Thurston could give him a hand now.

"Sheriff, you said before you don't have any deputies anymore. If the job's open, I'd like to apply for it."

Thurston stared up at Longarm. He couldn't seem to get any words out for a moment. Then he squeaked, "You, uh, you want to be my deputy?"

"That's right. I just got fired from the Box B, and I need some work."

Chapman spoke up. "That sounds like a good idea to

me, Sheriff. Mr. Parker strikes me as the capable sort."

"Yeah," muttered Thurston. "Yeah, but . . . bein' a lawman ain't easy. There's a whole lot o' responsibility . . . and the, uh, the public trust and such-like . . . I just ain't sure it'd work out, Parker."

Maybe Thurston was afraid that if he had a real deputy, he would have to work at being a real sheriff again. Or afraid that the citizens of the county would turn him out of office if they had a real alternative and pin the sheriff's badge on Longarm instead.

Of course, that would never happen, because Longarm already carried a badge for Uncle Sam. But Thurston didn't know that, and neither did anyone else in these parts.

Standing there and arguing wasn't going to do any good. Instead, Longarm nodded and said, "If you change your mind, just let me know, Sheriff. I reckon I'll be around town for a while."

"You're not moving on?" murmured Chapman.

"Not just yet."

And why was the professor so interested in his plans? Longarm wondered about that. If Chapman was mixed up with the outlaws, was even the Bloody Spaniard himself, then he wouldn't want anyone improving the law enforcement situation in Tascosa. Chapman had said that the sheriff always insisted on buying him a drink whenever he was in town. Maybe it was really the other way around and Chapman was the one promoting the friendship. Longarm figured Chapman might be able to worm all sorts of information, such as details of bank shipments and stagecoach schedules, out of Thurston without the sheriff even knowing what he was doing. It was something to think about.

Leaving the table, Longarm pushed the batwings aside and stepped out onto the boardwalk. He was at loose ends, unsure what to do next.

With a sigh, he went around the corner and down the alley to the lane at the rear of the buildings. He would go back upstairs to Arabella's room, he decided, and let her know that he would be able to accept her invitation to dinner after all. At least something good might come of this mess. Right now, though, he would just stay for a moment, so that he wouldn't disturb the paperwork she was doing—at least not too much, he hoped.

He started up the stairs, moving with quiet grace that was unusual in such a big man. When he reached the landing at the top, he put his hand on the doorknob, then stopped when he heard footsteps from the corridor inside. Arabella seemed to value discretion, so he waited until the footsteps faded away before he opened the door.

He went in, found the hall empty, and walked quickly to the door of Arabella's room. A soft knock brought an unexpectedly sharp response. The door was jerked open, as if she had been standing just on the other side of it. "What is it now?" Her eyes widened with surprise when she saw who her visitor was, and she said, "Oh. Custis. It's you."

"None other," said Longarm. "Is something wrong, Arabella?"

She shook her head. "No. No, of course not." She gave a little laugh. "I'm just a bit frustrated and impatient, trying to get all these numbers to balance when they stubbornly don't wish to."

Longarm didn't believe her. Her denial that anything was wrong had come too quickly, and before she had said that she had a good head for figures and seemed to almost be looking forward to doing the books.

Something else bothered him, too, but he couldn't put his finger on what it was. Something he had seen or heard . . .

"Do you want to come in?" asked Arabella, breaking into his thoughts.

"No, I won't keep you from your work," he said. "I just wanted to tell you that if that dinner invite still stands, I can accept now. I reckon I'm at loose ends."

"I thought you had to get back to the Box B."

"Barfield's downstairs," said Longarm. "He's riled at me, and he let me go. I figure Kellman's been trying to stir up hard feelings against me, and he finally succeeded."

"But that's foolish. Charley should know you're a loyal hand."

"I've only been around here a few days," Longarm pointed out. "Nobody really knows me all that well. Including you."

Her chin came up defiantly. "I know enough about you, Custis. And yes, certainly the dinner invitation still stands. Is eight o'clock all right?"

"I'll be here," he promised.

"Splendid." Arabella came up on her toes and leaned forward to brush a tantalizing kiss across Longarm's mouth. "I'll be looking forward to it all afternoon. Thinking of you will provide a welcome distraction from those ledger books."

"Don't let me distract you too much," Longarm told her with a grin. "You don't want to add up a column of numbers wrong and go in the hole."

"No. I daresay, you're the one who's going to be accomplishing part of that."

She closed the door while Longarm was still thinking about that, before the slow grin spread across his face.

He wound up in one of Tascosa's smaller saloons, playing poker all afternoon in a small-stakes game. Just so he wouldn't feel like he was completely wasting his time, he listened to the conversations going on around him and even steered them toward the Bloody Spaniard and the lawlessness that had spread through the area over the past weeks.

His interested perked up when one of his fellow card-players, a local storekeeper, said, "Nobody wants to talk much about that Spaniard thing, whatever it is. Not after what happened to young Brandywine."

"Who's that?" Longarm asked casually, even though he already knew the answer to the question.

"Fella who put out the newspaper here. After the Spaniard first popped up, Brandywine wrote a few stories about him. He claimed that he was going to find out who or what the Spaniard was, and that was going to make him famous and get him a job with *Harper's Weekly* or some big newspaper."

"But it didn't work out that way?"

"Nope. The young fool wound up slumped over his own printing press, a knife in his back."

That was mighty interesting, thought Longarm. It was the first real link he'd found between the Spaniard and one of the murder victims. Maybe Pete Brandywine *had* discovered the Spaniard's true identity—and gotten himself killed for his trouble. Taken along with the fact that Fletch McAuliffe might have been a competent deputy, it could mean that the killings weren't senseless after all, that the Bloody Spaniard had been eliminating men he considered to be threats to him.

That left the storekeeper, Hobart Rhone, and the three drifters. Longarm didn't know how they might have posed a threat to the Spaniard. But he wasn't through investigating the matter, either.

Nothing else productive came from the afternoon, unless it was the three dollars Longarm won playing poker. As it began to grow dark outside, he slipped the coins in his pocket, tossed off the last of the whiskey in the glass at his elbow, and stood up. "Much obliged for the game and the conversation, gents," he said to the men around the table.

He took his leave as the other players muttered their farewells. The sun was down, Longarm saw as he stepped outside, but a band of red still lingered along the western horizon. The afternoon heat lingered in the air as well. It would be several hours before things began to cool off. By morning, though, the air would be downright chilly.

He moved along an alley to the back lane and started along the rear of the buildings toward the Deuces. The gloom was even thicker back here, with shadows cloaking most of the area. It wouldn't lighten any until the moon rose. Longarm had always been able to see well in the dark, though, so he had no trouble finding his way. He reached the bottom of the stairs and started up.

He was halfway to the top when something made him pause. It was a sound, a faint *clank* that came from somewhere behind him, and as he started to turn his head, he saw something from the corner of his eye. A glow . . .

A glowing figure, in fact, emerging from the shadows as if from the mists of time itself. Longarm stiffened as he saw the armored shape standing there, one arm raised. Longarm reached for his gun, his hand moving across his body toward the Colt in the cross-draw rig.

The Spaniard's lifted arm dropped, as if in a signal.

And all hell broke loose in the dark alley behind the Deuces, orange muzzle flame blooming garishly in the shadows as guns began to roar.

Chapter 16

Longarm threw himself backward on the stairs as slugs chewed splinters from the risers. He triggered two fast shots at the muzzle flashes, not really hoping to hit any of the bushwhackers but wanting to show them that he had fangs, maybe make a couple of them duck for cover. Then he launched in a roll toward the edge of the stairs.

The staircase had a railing on its outer edge, supported by thin boards every few feet. Longarm hit those boards hard. Some of them broke, and others pulled loose with a screech of nails. He rolled right off the stairs and dropped toward the ground.

It wasn't a very long fall, no more than eight or nine feet. He landed in a crouch and went on down to one knee as bullets continued to thud into the building behind him. So far he hadn't been hit, but with all the lead flying around, that luck couldn't last forever.

He snapped another shot into the shadows where the bushwhackers were hidden, then surged to his feet and dashed toward the corner of the building. As he ran, he looked for the glowing golden figure who had ordered the shooting to start. Spotting the ghostly shape, he fired on the run. But the Bloody Spaniard crabbed sideways, moving awkwardly in the armor, and then vanished, fading away like the phantom he seemed to be.

A slug whistled past Longarm's head as he threw himself around the corner of the Deuces. He heard shouts from the street and from inside the building as people reacted to the commotion of gunfire. He pressed his back to the wall and thumbed fresh cartridges into the empty chambers of his gun as he waited to see if the ambushers were going to come after him.

Instead, after a few moments of silence he heard a sudden rattle of hoofbeats that faded into the distance. The hidden gunmen had fled. Longarm wondered if the Spaniard was with them . . . or if the man who wore that golden armor was still here in Tascosa.

"Is . . . is anybody there?"

The high-pitched, quavery, frightened voice calling the question down the alley belonged to Sheriff Thurston. Longarm was a little surprised the lawman had stirred his stumps enough to come investigate the outbreak of shooting.

"Take it easy, Sheriff," replied Longarm. "It's me, Custis Parker."

"What's goin' on back there? Don't try nothin', I got a scattergun."

Longarm stepped away from the wall and started toward the street. "Didn't you hear me? I said—"

"Damn it, drop that gun! I'll shoot!"

Longarm heard the panic in the sheriff's voice. Thurston's bulky figure was silhouetted against the glow of the lights along the street, and Longarm saw him lift the shotgun in his hands. Acting instinctively, Longarm threw himself forward just as Thurston touched off both barrels of the greener.

The deafening double roar filled the close confines of the alley and beat against Longarm's ears like a fist. Twin plumes of flame gushed from the barrels of the shotgun and for an instant lit the scene like a flash of hellfire. Longarm hugged the ground as the double charge of buckshot ripped through the air above him. Luckily, the range was close enough so that the loads hadn't spread out much by the time they reached him. The deadly pellets all missed him, but if he hadn't hit the dirt, they would have torn him in half.

He was up instantly, bounding forward to grab the barrels of the shotgun and wrest it out of Thurston's hands. "You damned fool!" shouted Longarm, unable to contain his anger. "You almost killed me!"

The sheriff, quaking with fear, backed away as several townspeople came up behind him. "I . . . I thought you was one o' them owlhoots!" he cried. "You back off now, mister! I . . . I'm the law around here!"

"And a piss-poor excuse for it, if you ask me," snapped Longarm. He threw the empty scattergun at Thurston's feet.

"You shouldn't oughta talk to me like that." Thurston sounded like his dignity was wounded. "I come to see what all the shootin' was about, didn't I?"

"Yeah, I suppose so," Longarm said grudgingly. He saw Lady Arabella Winthrop among the bystanders. She had come out of the Deuces. "Somebody tried to kill me while I was walking behind the saloon," he went on, opting for discretion instead of mentioning that he had been on his way up the rear stairs for his rendezvous with Arabella.

"I told you," said Thurston. "I told you, Parker. You've made the trouble around here even worse."

"Damn it, *I'm* the one who got shot at."

"Yeah, well, maybe if you'd leave town, people would stop shootin' at you."

From Thurston's point of view, what he was saying might make sense. It just made Longarm mad. He reined in his temper and said, "I'm not going anywhere."

"But you said Charley Barfield fired you. You got no reason to hang around here makin' life harder for folks.'

"Harder for lawmen who don't do their jobs, you mean." Longarm gave an abrupt shake of his head and turned away. He wasn't going to waste any more time standing around arguing with the sheriff. He brushed past Thurston and headed for the front door of the Deuces. "I need a drink."

Now that the show, such as it was, was over, the crowd broke up and people went on about their business. Arabella put a hand on Longarm's arm and went into the saloon with him. "Are you all right?" she asked anxiously.

"Yeah. A lot of lead went flying around, but none of it hit me. Reckon I was lucky."

"Maybe the sheriff was right. Maybe you should leave Tascosa. It seems you encounter trouble everywhere you turn."

Longarm looked over at her. "Is that what you want? You want me to get out of town, too?"

She hesitated, but only for a second. Then she shook her head and smiled. "No. That's not what I want at all. I think you know what I want, Custis." She linked her arm with his. "And I don't care who knows it."

To his surprise, she marched him across the room toward the stairs, calling to one of the bartenders to bring dinner and a bottle of brandy up to her room. From the way the men in the saloon watched in envious surprise, Longarm figured this sort of thing didn't happen too often, if ever. The lady wasn't the sort to bestow her favors indiscriminately.

He wasn't going to argue with her, though. Between getting shot at and constantly running into a brick wall in his investigation, he was ready for some relaxation. He went up the stairs with Arabella, trying not to grin too much.

• • •

The brandy and glasses arrived almost right away, the trays of food a short time later. When they had finished eating, Longarm sat down in a wing chair and stretched his legs out in front of him. He had a snifter of brandy in one hand, a cheroot in the other, and a beautiful woman perched on an arm of the chair, stroking his forehead with smooth, cool fingertips. Despite all the problems he had encountered since coming to the Panhandle, at that moment he was remarkably content. He closed his eyes and sighed.

"I'm glad you didn't leave town," said Arabella as she leaned closer to him. "You're a remarkable man, Custis. Tascosa hasn't seen the likes of you for quite some time."

"You're flattering me too much," he told her with an amused chuckle. "Not that I'm saying you should stop or anything."

She kissed his forehead. "Just in case you do leave town, I want to give you something to remember me by."

Longarm didn't think it was likely he would forget her anytime soon, but if she wanted to do even more, he wasn't going to tell her not to. Instead he sipped the brandy and smoked the cheroot as she stood up and began to slowly take off her clothes.

Watching a beautiful woman strip was one of the prettiest sights in the world, he thought. He felt himself stiffening as Arabella reached behind her to undo the fasteners of her dress and then let it fall forward. She wiggled it and her petticoats down over her hips and stepped out of them, leaving her in bloomers and a corset. Her breasts were bare, and the large brown nipples that crowned the creamy globes were already erect. She peeled down the bloomers, revealing lush thighs and the triangle of fine-spun dark hair between them. Leaving the corset on, she cupped her breasts for a moment, stroking the hard nipples as she walked toward Longarm. By now his shaft was as hard as a bar of iron, tenting up the front of his trousers.

151

Arabella knelt between his knees and reached forward to deftly unfasten the buttons that held him in. She undid his belt as well and opened his trousers. At her urging, he lifted his hips and let her pull the trousers and the long underwear down so that his erection sprang free. The long, thick pole jutted up proudly from his groin.

She licked her lips as she wrapped both hands around his manhood and slid them up and down, milking a pearl of moisture from the opening at the tip. Using a finger, she spread the dew around the head. Then, as Longarm's teeth clenched on the cheroot and his grip on the stem of the snifter tightened, Arabella leaned forward and began to lick all around the crown of his shaft.

British she might be, but she spoke French mighty fluently, he thought as for long minutes she continued to lick and kiss up and down the entire length of his pole. She reached between his legs with one hand and cupped the heavy sac that hung underneath his member, gently rolling the globes back and forth in her palm. Just when he thought he couldn't stand any more of the exquisite torment she was handing out to him, she licked all the way up the underside of his shaft, starting at the bottom and ending at the tip. Her red lips parted, and she took him into her mouth.

Longarm almost shot off then and there, but he forced himself to control the reaction. Arabella skillfully clamped her hand around the base of his shaft to help him delay his climax. She opened her mouth wider, but even so, she could take in only a small portion of his massive organ. Her tongue slithered around the head as she began to suck.

Watching his shaft disappear between her lips was an incredibly arousing sight. He groaned around the cheroot and suppressed the impulse to thrust deeper into her mouth. Arabella was excited, too. She kept one hand around his manhood to steady it while she used the other to reach between her legs and rub herself. Longarm would have been glad to do that, had he been in a position to do so, but under the circumstances he couldn't move, couldn't do anything except sit there and luxuriate in the waves of pure pleasure her oral caresses sent cascading through him.

He could only last so long. He set the snifter aside on a table and tangled his fingers in her dark hair as her head bobbed up and down over his groin. In a voice that was hoarse and strained from passion, he said, "If you want to move this to the bed—"

She shook her head without letting his shaft slip out of her mouth. The side-to-side movement was an added bit of enjoyment.

"Then it ain't going to be much longer," he warned her breathlessly.

She nodded in understanding and sucked harder.

If that was what she wanted, thought Longarm, he was more than happy to oblige.

He closed his eyes and let himself go. His shaft swelled even more in her grip and began to throb as his climax boiled up its length. Like a volcano erupting, his seed exploded, gushing forth in thick, white-hot spurts. The muscles in Arabella's throat worked as she tried to swallow what he gave her, but she couldn't keep up with the flood. Some of it escaped and ran down the sides of her mouth onto her chin. She pulled back with a gasp, and the last couple of drops landed on her cheek.

A long, heartfelt sigh escaped from Longarm's lips. Every muscle in his body was relaxed. His mind was clear and calm, his thoughts drifting lazily in the lassitude that followed culmination.

And that was when a thought came to him, a thought so incredible, so unbelievable, that at first he almost discarded it without any consideration. But the idea was insistent. He inhaled deeply on the cheroot, blew out the smoke. Crazy, sure, he told himself, but it wasn't impossible. It just might be true . . .

"Custis?"

He opened his eyes and looked down at Arabella. She leaned against one of his legs, her head pillowed on the thigh.

"What's wrong?" she asked. "You suddenly looked like you were a million miles away."

"Nope." He reached down and stroked her glossy dark hair. Under the circumstances, it wouldn't be very polite to tell her that instead of thinking about what she had just done for him, he had been considering the facts of the case. Nor did he want to say anything about the wild theory that had just occurred to him, not until he had more to go on than pure supposition. "I was just figuring that it's your turn now."

She came smoothly to her feet and turned to walk over to the bed. The white cheeks of her rump jiggled enticingly under the corset. She stretched, lay down on her stomach, and then rolled over and spread her legs to reveal the pink cleft between her thighs. "I think that's an excellent idea," she said throatily.

Longarm stood up, quickly peeled off the rest of his clothes, and went to kneel next to the bed. He had some more investigating to do, but it could wait until morning, he thought as he leaned forward and used his thumbs to part the fleshy pink lips of Arabella's sex.

Right now he had something to investigate that was more interesting and less dangerous . . . at least most of the time.

Chapter 17

Sometime along toward morning, a rumble of thunder in the distance roused Longarm from sleep. He opened his eyes but didn't lift his head from the pillow. Arabella lay beside him, her dark hair spread out around her head. They snuggled together spoon-fashion, nude, her bottom pressed warmly against his groin.

He heard the thunder again, saw the faint flicker of lightning against the curtains. It rained more often here in the Panhandle than it did in some places, but by and large this was a pretty arid region. The ranchers would probably be glad for a shower if it didn't rain so hard that it all ran off without soaking in. In a downpour, all those dry washes that cut across the landscape could fill up in a hurry.

For the moment, though, the storm was still a long way off. He held Arabella a little tighter and dozed off again.

They made love again when they woke up in the morning, a slow, sensuous coupling, and it occurred to Longarm that for the second day in a row, he was starting his day by romping with a beautiful woman. Rosalinda Hernandez and Lady Arabella Winthrop were quite different in all respects except one: They were both lovely.

Most fellas would think he was mighty lucky, he mused after his climax had drained him and he lay there between Arabella's widespread thighs, his softening member still buried inside her. He never seemed to have any trouble winding up between the sheets with beautiful gals. But a month never passed when he didn't get shot at a dozen times or more. Any hombres who might be jealous of him had to consider *that,* too.

In fact, it was likely he would be shot at again before this day was over, because at last he had a good hunch who was in the glowing armor of the Bloody Spaniard.

"Are you leaving, Custis?" murmured Arabella sleepily as he rolled off of her.

"I'm not leaving town yet," he told her. He nuzzled her ear and stroked one of her breasts. "But I reckon I'll ride out for a while, maybe take a look around."

"Tell the cook to prepare breakfast for you." Arabella rolled onto her side and closed her eyes. "I'm going back to sleep. This is early for me."

He patted her rump and then slid out of bed. "All right, darlin'. Enjoy your rest."

He dressed quickly and quietly and left the room. Since Arabella had taken him up to her room so openly the night before, he didn't worry about compromising her reputation by going down the stairs into the saloon's big main room. The Deuces had only a few customers at this hour. A couple of men drank at the bar, and a desultory poker game went on at one of the tables. Otherwise the place was empty.

Only one bartender was on duty. Longarm asked him for coffee and something to eat, and the man nodded. "Comin' right up, Mr. Parker."

"Sheriff been in this morning?" asked Longarm.

"Thurston?" Scorn dripped from the bartender's voice. "I haven't seen him. He's probably over at Maude's whorehouse."

"What about that Professor Chapman?"

The bartender shook his head. "Nope. I think he headed out of town yesterday afternoon. He never stays around for very long at a time."

Longarm nodded slowly. He asked the bartender to bring the coffee and food over to one of the tables when it was ready, and the man agreed. Longarm sat down and lit a cheroot, then smoked until his breakfast arrived.

When he was finished with the meal, he dug out a coin and left it on the table to pay for the food and coffee, even though he figured Arabella had intended for it to be on the house. He wanted to pay his own way, though. As he fished out another cheroot, he pushed through the batwings and stepped onto the boardwalk in front of the saloon.

There was no sunshine over the Panhandle today. Thick gray clouds scudded through the skies. The street was still dry and dusty, though. The rainstorm hadn't gotten here. When Longarm looked to the west, he saw that the clouds were darker there. Tiny fingers of lightning traced through them, followed long moments later by the faint rolling boom of thunder. Distances were deceptive out here, Longarm knew. That storm was probably a good thirty or forty miles away, and it seemed to be just sitting there, not coming any closer. It was possible Tascosa wouldn't see a drop out of those clouds.

Longarm didn't want to go back to Maude's to roust out Sheriff Thurston. There was no real reason for him to do such a thing. His theory was still just that—a theory. He needed evidence. Instead he walked along the street until he reached the general store belonging to one of the men he had played poker with the day before, the one who had talked about the newspaperman, Pete Brandywine.

"Mornin'," Longarm said with a nod to the storekeeper, who stood behind the counter wearing a canvas apron.

The man looked a little surprised to see him, but he returned the nod and the greeting. Longarm put his hands flat on the counter and went on, "I reckon you know most of the other businessmen in town."

"Sure. I've been here in Tascosa for a couple of years, so I know just about everybody in these parts."

"You knew Hobart Rhone?"

"Of course. It was a terrible thing, what happened to him."

There were no customers in the store at the moment, and Longarm sensed the proprietor would be pretty talkative if he was prodded just a mite. "What did happen to him? I never heard the details."

The storekeeper evidently didn't wonder how Longarm knew about Rhone's death at all. As far as he knew, Longarm had only been around Tascosa for a few days. Instead, with a shake of his head, he answered, "He was beaten to death in the back room of his own store." He pointed. "Right there across the street. I heard the yelling that morning when the kid who swept out the place for him came in and found him. Went right over to see what was wrong. It was terrible. Somebody had taken a whip to Hobart and then caved in his head with the butt end of it. Just terrible."

"The two of you get along all right, what with you being competitors and all?"

The storekeeper's eyebrows arched. "What? Of course we did! Hobart was a friend of mine. If you're implying—"

Longarm raised his hands, palms out, to forestall the protest. "Nope, not at all. Didn't mean any offense, old son. I was just wondering, that's all."

The man frowned. "Why are you asking all these questions, anyway?"

"Curious, is all." Longarm lowered his voice to a more conspiratorial tone, hoping to repair the damage. "I heard something about that so-called Bloody Spaniard having something to do with Rhone's murder."

The storekeeper sniffed. "The day that Hobart's body was found, a couple of people claimed to have seen the Spaniard lurking around the back of the store the night before. They were just drunks, though. I think they imagined the whole thing."

"Drunks, eh?"

"Yes. In fact, they wound up dead not long after—" The man stopped short, his eyes widening. "Wait a minute. You reckon there could be any connection?"

"You tell me," said Longarm. He had come in here to see if he could find some link between the murdered Hobart Rhone and the man he suspected of being the Bloody Spaniard, but so far he had drawn a blank. However, he might have stumbled onto something else.

"Maybe they *did* see something," the storekeeper said. "Maybe the Spaniard came back to finish them off later. He was too late, though. They had already spread the rumor about seeing him all over town."

The man had switched sides in a hurry, scoffing at the notion of the Bloody Spaniard a moment earlier, now seeming to accept the possibility that somebody in glowing armor was clanking around Tascosa killing people. But that was just human nature, thought Longarm. People were quick to grasp at the mysterious and the intriguing.

"But nobody ever found any reason for Rhone to have been killed?"

The storekeeper waved a hand. "Oh, Sheriff Thurston poked around Hobart's place and said something about maybe there was a robbery. He thought somebody had broken in and that Hobart caught the thief there. But I think Thurston was just grasping at straws and looking for an excuse not to investigate further. That would have been too much work." The man sighed and shook his head. "Hobart would have been really disappointed if he'd seen the way Thurston handled everything."

"Oh? How's that?"

"Hobart was the one who suggested Thurston run for sheriff in the first place. Back then they were friends. But when he was killed, Thurston didn't really do a damned thing about it."

"Yeah, I've noticed he ain't much when it comes to enforcing the law," Longarm said dryly. "He's pretty much over his head when it comes to all the trouble that's been going on around here."

The storekeeper snorted in contempt. "You can say that again. Everybody's scared of that damned Bloody Spaniard, business is bad, ranches are losing cattle right and left, and the manager of the stagecoach line is talking about cutting out the run that comes through here because of all the robberies. If this keeps up, Tascosa is liable to dry up and blow away."

"Well, maybe it won't come to that."

The door opened and a couple of women in bonnets came in. The storekeeper looked at them and asked Longarm, "Anything else I can do for you?"

"Nope, I reckon not. Thanks for the conversation."

The man grunted. "I'd be careful if I was you," he said, lowering his voice so the two ladies couldn't hear. "The last fella who came around here asking so many questions wound up dead, just like those drunks."

Longarm's interest quickened. "Is that so?"

"That's right. He rode into town, started asking questions, and somebody shot him that night, dumped his body in an alley. Curiosity killed the cat, I reckon."

"Curiosity?" murmured Longarm. "Or the Bloody Spaniard?"

The storekeeper just gave him a look and then went along the counter to wait on the two women.

Longarm sauntered out of the store. He had come in hoping to find out one thing and had discovered several other possibilities. Those two murdered drunks could have seen something that might identify the Bloody Spaniard. And the third man had been asking questions about the ghostly figure, too. Could he have been some sort of detective or lawman working undercover, much like Longarm himself? There had been an attempt on his life the night before, he thought. He had narrowly avoided becoming the Spaniard's seventh victim.

It was all coming together in his mind, the disjointed suspicions forming into one whole, a theory that was farfetched but still made sense and would explain most of what had happened around here. All he had to do was prove it and then confront the man behind all the mysterious, deadly events.

He wasn't going to have a chance to do that now, however, because more trouble rode into Tascosa at that moment. The rattle of hoofbeats made Longarm look up. He saw a man riding hard along the street, swaying in the saddle. Blood stained the rider's shirt. He saw Longarm and hauled back on the reins, trying to bring his horse to a stop, but he was too weak to stay in the saddle. As he toppled to the ground, Longarm leaped off the boardwalk and raced to the fallen man's side.

Longarm knelt in the dusty street to lift Alejandro Carranza's head and rest it on his leg. "Alejandro!" he said urgently to the wounded old-timer. "What happened?"

"S-Señor Parker . . ." gasped Alejandro. "They . . . they took her! Rosalinda! She is gone!"

"Who?" asked Longarm, leaning over the old man. "Who took her?"

"B-Barfield's . . . men . . . from the Box B . . ."

A crowd gathered around, drawn by the sight of the wounded man lying in the street. Longarm glanced up and snapped, "Somebody fetch a sawbones." Then he looked back at Alejandro and said gently, "Tell me what happened."

161

Alejandro drew a deep breath, wincing as fresh pain shot through him. His shirt was wet with blood on the right side. Longarm didn't know how bad the injury was, but at Alejandro's age, any bullet wound could prove fatal, just from the shock and loss of blood. But the old man seemed to gather some strength, and his voice was steadier as he said, "Very early this morning, just after Ramon and I had come in from patrolling the ranch, someone set the hay in our barn on fire. Ramon and I saw the smoke and ran to try to put out the flames . . . but as we came out of the house, they shot at us." Alejandro shuddered. "Ramon was hit, and then me. I tried to drag him into the house, but the gringos cut us off. We had to hide in the barn. The smoke and the heat, they were bad, so bad . . . but we had our guns and kept the men from getting inside the barn. Then . . . then they circled the house and went in after Rosalinda . . . There was more shooting . . ."

"Was she hurt?" asked Longarm.

The old man gave a weak shake of his head. "I . . . I do not think so. I saw him drag her out of the house and put her on a horse, and she was still struggling. I saw no blood on her."

"Who did it?" Longarm's jaw was tight with anger as he asked the question. "Who had her? Barfield?"

"No . . . It was the other man . . . Kellman . . . He led them . . ."

Arch Kellman. Longarm had never trusted him, and rightly so. "Were the others with him Box B men?"

"*S-Sí.* I recognized them."

"How many?"

"Four . . . that I saw."

So five men from Barfield's spread, led by Arch Kellman, had raided the Hernandez ranch. That didn't mean Barfield himself had ordered the raid or even that he had known about it. But things didn't look good for the burly cattleman, either. Out here on the frontier, men had been strung up on less evidence.

He could get to the bottom of that later, Longarm told himself. Right now the important thing was to get Rosa out of Kellman's hands before anything else happened to her.

The crowd parted as a couple of men pushed their way through. One of them, Longarm saw to his surprise, was Sheriff Thurston, who was up and around earlier than usual. The other was a white-haired, middle-aged man with a black bag in his hand.

"Back off, folks!" ordered Thurston. "Give the doc some room."

The medico knelt on Alejandro's other side and said to Longarm, "Lay him down, carefully." Longarm did so, and the doctor began cutting away the wounded man's shirt, peeling it back to reveal the bullet hole in Alejandro's side. To Longarm's relief, the wound, though messy, didn't appear too serious. The bullet had ripped through flesh, but only shallowly. Chances were it had missed any vital organs.

The doctor confirmed as much with a quick examination. "Some of you men pick him up and carry him to my office," he ordered briskly. "He should be all right if he hasn't lost too much blood."

Longarm stood in the street for a moment and watched Alejandro being taken away to the doctor's office. Then he turned toward the livery stable, intending to get his horse and set off after Kellman and the other men who had raided the Eagle Ranch.

"Wait just a minute," said Thurston, stopping him. "What the hell happened here?"

Longarm regarded him narrowly. "Are you actually going to act like a lawman for once, Sheriff? If you want, I reckon you can gather up a posse. Rosalinda Hernandez has been kidnapped."

Thurston's eyes widened. "K-Kidnapped?" he repeated. "By who?"

"Arch Kellman and some other riders from the Box B."

"Dadgummit, that don't sound like somethin' Charley Barfield would do."

"Maybe Barfield didn't have anything to do with it. We won't know until we catch up to Kellman."

"You, uh, you volunteerin' to take charge of the posse?"

Longarm frowned. "Is that what you want?"

"Yesterday you asked for a deputy's job. Now you got one, if you still want it. I'm deputizin' you to go after Kellman."

Longarm gave him a curt nod. "Sure. I'll take it."

"You want a badge?"

"No, just spread the word that I'll be riding out in ten minutes. Any man who wants to ride with me is welcome—but I'm in charge."

"Sure, sure. I'll see that ever'body understands. Thanks, Parker." Thurston pulled a dirty bandanna from his pocket and mopped sweat off his face. "No offense, but I swear you attract more trouble than any hombre I ever saw. First you get bushwhacked on them stairs behind the Deuces last night, and now that old Mex rides into town covered with blood and falls right at your feet. How come that always happens to you, Parker?"

"Just lucky, I reckon," Longarm said grimly.

Chapter 18

It was closer to fifteen minutes before Longarm rode out of Tascosa, but when he did, it was at the head of a group of fifteen men. Most of them were cowboys from the various ranches in the area who happened to have been in town when they heard that a posse was being formed. These wild young riders weren't going to pass up the chance for some excitement. The rest of the posse was made up of businessmen from Tascosa who felt it was their duty to pitch in.

Longarm had stopped by the doctor's office and spoken briefly again to Alejandro Carranza, who still clung to consciousness. Alejandro told him that he had gotten the wounded Ramon into the house after the raiders galloped off with Rosa. The old-timer wasn't sure how badly Ramon was wounded, but the young man had been unconscious, and Alejandro had known that he couldn't wait for Ramon to wake up. He'd had to get to town and seek help, so that a rescue party could set off after Rosa and her kidnappers as soon as possible.

Longarm promised Alejandro that they would tend to Ramon. Then he'd left the doctor's office, swung up into the saddle, and galloped out of town with the other members of the posse.

The only logical place to start was the Hernandez ranch. They could pick up the trail of the raiders there. As the posse approached the place around mid-morning, Longarm wondered if they would find Ramon Hernandez dead or alive. It was entirely possible the young man had succumbed to his wounds after Alejandro rode off.

The adobe walls of the barn hadn't burned, of course, but the inside was gutted by fire and the roof had collapsed, Longarm saw as he and his companions rode up to the ranch headquarters. He dismounted and hurried into the house. As he did, more thunder growled in the west. The clouds in that direction were black now, possibly appearing a little darker than they actually were because the sun peeked through the overcast in the east and shone on them.

Ramon lay on the divan, a blanket hastily thrown over him. Sweat beaded his face, and his chest rose and fell raggedly as he breathed. Even though Ramon didn't like him, Longarm was glad to see that the youngster was still alive. He peeled the blanket back, saw bloodstains on Ramon's chest, right arm, and left leg.

A couple of the men from Tascosa had come into the room behind Longarm. One of them commented, "Looks like they pert near shot him to pieces."

"Maybe it ain't quite as bad as it looks," said Longarm. "Either of you fellas know anything about patching up bullet wounds?" He had considerable experience along those lines himself, but he didn't want to take the time necessary to stay here and tend to Ramon's injuries. Not while Arch Kellman was holding Rosa prisoner.

"I've done a mite of horse doctorin'," said the other man. He was broad-shouldered and had huge, callused hands scarred by his work as a blacksmith. But those hands were surprisingly gentle and deft as he knelt by the divan and started examining Ramon's wounds.

Longarm clapped a hand on the blacksmith's shoulder. "We're going to leave you here to take care of him, then," he said. "Patch him up as best you can, then get him back to town."

The blacksmith nodded. "Sure. Wish I could get a crack at the bastards who done this, though. It ain't right to shoot a fella and carry off his sister, even if they're Mexicans."

"We'll get in a few licks for you, Tully," said the other townie.

Longarm strode outside and swung up onto the buckskin. Finding the tracks left by the raiders took only a few minutes. The trail led south.

"This is the way to Barfield's spread," one of the cowboys pointed out as the posse rode.

Longarm nodded. "I know." He was a mite surprised that Kellman was heading so openly toward the home ranch.

A while later, he reined in where more tracks crossed the ones they were following. His experienced eyes read the sign with no trouble. A sizable jag of cattle had been driven across here, and Kellman and the rest of the raiders had stopped momentarily to talk to the men who were driving the herd. Then Kellman and his companions had moved on toward Barfield's ranch.

Longarm waved his companions on, a suspicion growing in his mind as he did so. Maybe this was the big cleanup at last, the grand finale to the symphony of lawlessness that had been playing in the Panhandle for the past few months. Those cattle on their way west to the New Mexico line were probably what was left of the Hernandez herd. The rustlers had made a clean sweep, and their rendezvous with Kellman proved, at least to Longarm's satisfaction, that the saturnine gun thrower had been part of the gang all along.

And now that he thought about what had happened in Tascosa this morning, Longarm was sure beyond a shadow of a doubt who the leader of that gang was. The final piece of the puzzle had fallen into place.

A short time later, he spotted a plume of smoke rising in the distance. One of the other men noticed it as well and called out, "Hey, that smoke looks like it's coming from Barfield's place!"

Longarm wasn't a bit surprised by that development. He pushed on at an even faster pace, the rest of the posse trailing along behind him.

The column of smoke grew blacker and thicker and taller. When the posse reached the headquarters of the Box B, Longarm saw that all the buildings were ablaze. Bodies lay scattered around the place. His face bleak and hard, Longarm dismounted and hurried to each of the fallen men in turn, hoping to find a sign of life. They were all dead, though, including Charley Barfield himself. The big cattleman lay on his face, a six-gun near his out-flung hand where he had dropped it as he fell. Longarm rolled Barfield onto his back and saw that the rancher had at least six bullet holes in him. Someone had taken savage pleasure in ventilating Barfield. Longarm suspected it had been Kellman.

A groan from the direction of the burning cook shack caught Longarm's attention. He sprang up and ran toward the shack, ducking through the open door. He heard another groan, and in the thick smoke that filled the little structure, that helped him find the man slumped on the floor, where there was still a little breathable air. Longarm grabbed him under the arms and dragged him out into the open just before the roof of the shack fell in.

The wounded man was old Rosebud, the cook. He had been shot, and he was badly burned. But he blinked his eyes open and looked up at Longarm, coughed and said, "P-Parker? What're you . . . doin' . . . h-here?"

"I'm leading a posse that's after the men who did this, Rosebud," Longarm told the old-timer. "It was Kellman, wasn't it?"

"Y-Yeah . . . that crazy . . . son of a bitch! Him and . . . half a dozen more polecats . . . who turned on Charley . . ."

That tied in with what Longarm had suspected for quite a while now. Kellman was one of the outlaws, and he had recruited some of Barfield's riders to the owlhoot cause. They had formed a festering sore here on the Box B, and Barfield hadn't even been aware of it until too late. Chances were, rustlers were swooping in elsewhere on the ranch right now, gathering up all the stock they could and driving it before them toward New Mexico. If the wide-loopers had their way, before the day was over they would have made one of the biggest hauls in the history of the West.

Longarm was going to have something to say about that, however. He figured that he and the posse would be outnumbered, but they had to push on anyway, had to catch up to Kellman and the others before they got the stolen herd across the border.

Rosebud's gnarled hand clawed at Longarm's sleeve. "You go . . . get them dirty sons . . . You get 'em . . . good . . ." The hand fell away.

"Bet a hat on it, old-timer," said Longarm, even though Rosebud was beyond hearing him now. He lowered the old man's head to the ground and then stood up, wondering how St. Peter liked his biscuits.

One of the cowboys came up to Longarm. "We gonna bury these boys?" he asked solemnly.

Longarm shook his head. "I wish we could, but there's no time, and we can't afford to split up. We're all going after the ones who done this."

"That's fine by us, Parker," said the cowboy with a curt

nod. Anger glittered in his eyes, anger at the savage slaughter that had taken place here.

There was something else Longarm wanted to do before they rode out, though. He said, "The name's Long."

The cowboy frowned. "What?"

Longarm raised his voice so that all the other members of the posse could hear him. "It's time you fellas knew that my name is really Custis Long. I'm a deputy United States marshal from Denver. I've been working under-cover for the last few days around here, trying to bust up the gang that's been raising so much hell."

"You mean the Bloody Spaniard's bunch?" called out another man.

"That's right. I know there are rumors about him being a ghost, but I'm here to tell you that he's not. He's flesh and blood, just like you and me, and he's one of the sli-ckest owlhoots I've ever run across. But we're going to put an end to his outfit today."

Longarm had a reason for revealing his true identity. Later, when they caught up to the gang, they would be outnumbered and some of the men might hesitate about getting into a fight with them. They would be more likely to show some grit if they knew they were being led into battle by a federal lawman.

As if to confirm that, one of the men said loudly, "We're with you, Marshal. Let's go get those murderin', rustlin' bastards!"

Longarm grabbed the saddle horn and swung up onto the buckskin. He grinned tightly at the men around him. "There's an old saying about Texans being tough enough to charge Hades with a bucket of water," he said. "Damned if I don't believe it."

Thunder rolled and lightning flickered almost constantly in the cloud-choked sky ahead of them, but the air was utterly still and so dry that Longarm was convinced he saw sparks dancing around the ears of his horse a time or two. For the past hour, he had smelled the dust that hung in the air, dust kicked up by the passage of hundreds of stolen cattle. The trail led west from the Box B headquarters, straight toward the New Mexico line. Once across the border, the outlaws would be beyond the reach of Texas law.

They didn't know they had a federal star packer after them. Longarm wouldn't let such a boundary line stop him if it came to that. But since he was down here in the Panhandle lending a hand to the Texas Rangers, it would be better if he could corral the skunks before they crossed over into New Mexico with their loot-on-the-hoof.

Longarm wasn't sure just how big the stolen herd was. It was entirely possible that by now the stock stolen from the Hernandez ranch had been merged with the Box B cows. There could be as many as a thousand head, he estimated. In a way, that was good. With a herd that big, the thieves could only push along so fast. Longarm and the posse could make better time.

He kept the pace as fast as he could, pausing only when it was necessary to rest the posse's horses. Riding their mounts to death wouldn't accomplish anything. Those breaks were short, and soon the men were back in their saddles.

The storm worried him. He kept a watchful eye on the dark clouds as they scudded through the heavens. The rain seemed to be stalled over to the west right now, but that situation could change quickly.

The smell of the dust grew stronger. A few minutes later, Longarm sighted the dust cloud itself, roiling up a couple of miles ahead of them. He leaned forward in the saddle, a new urgency gripping him. "Come on!" he called to the men with him. "They're not far ahead of us now!"

The posse surged forward, asking their horses to respond with yet another burst of energy. The gallant animals did their best. Longarm's buckskin had more sand than most, so he drew a little ahead of the others.

Suddenly, a puff of cool wind hit him in the face.

The wind brought with it a new smell—the unmistakable scent of rain. Thunder boomed. The sky began to grow darker by the minute as Longarm galloped ahead. Whatever force of nature had been holding back the storm had relented at last and given it free rein to come boiling across the flat Texas landscape. Longarm hoped there were no twisters within that maelstrom of clouds. The last thing they needed now was a tornado.

He spotted a dark, broad, low-lying mass ahead of him at the base of the dust cloud. That was the stolen herd, he thought. After another moment, he began to be able to make out the shapes of riders moving behind the herd, chousing it on toward the west and the New Mexico line. Longarm wasn't sure where they were. It wasn't like the border between Texas and Mexico. There was no Rio Grande to form an unmistakable dividing line. For all he knew, they might already be in New Mexico Territory, but he didn't think that was the case.

He didn't really care, either. He was finally closing in on the men he was after, and he wasn't going to stop now.

Someone with the herd must have spotted the pursuers, because several men abruptly peeled off and turned back, heading toward the posse at full speed. Longarm saw the orange winking of muzzle flashes as the rustlers opened fire. He slid his Winchester from its sheath and guided the horse with his knees as he brought the rifle to his shoulder and threw lead back at the owlhoots.

A huge clap of thunder shook the earth, making the shots seem puny by comparison. The flash of lightning was a thousand times brighter than the burst of flame from a gun muzzle. Man's squabbles were as nothing when measured against the fury of the storm that was now rushing across the prairie toward them. But to Longarm and the other men engaged in battle, nothing was more important than surviving the next few minutes. Longarm's Winchester ripped out seven shots as fast as he could cock and fire, and he saw two of the rustlers tumble from their saddles. The other outlaws turned and fled as the posse gave chase, still firing after them.

Another rumbling explosion of thunder sounded overhead. Large drops of rain smacked against Longarm's face. There were only a few drops so far, but they fell hard and heavy. The wind gusted, kicking up more sand and grit. It would have to rain a lot to lay that dust.

As the thunder died down for a moment, Longarm heard another rumbling sound. It took him only a second to recognize it. The sound was a mixture of thousands of hooves pounding the ground and frightened bawls coming from the throats of hundreds of cattle. Longarm had been on enough cattle drives, had helped to push enough herds up the trails from Texas to the Kansas railheads, back in the old days not long after the war. He knew what was going to happen next, knew it was as inevitable as the rising of the sun.

Sure enough, the spooked herd stampeded.

One second, though spread out and moving fast, the herd was still under control. The next instant, it was a wild thing bolting straight ahead in sheer panic. Longarm saw some of the rustlers on the flanks trying to keep the herd bunched. They failed miserably as the frantic cattle began to spread out and run in every direction. The outlaws tried to veer their horses away. Some succeeded, but others were engulfed by the herd. Any time man and horse went down in such a situation, that was the end for them. No one could live through the carnage of hooves and horns.

Longarm wondered where Kellman and Rosa were. He was confident that Kellman would have kept the prisoner with him. If they had been out in front of the herd when it stampeded . . .

Longarm didn't want to think about that.

Instead he pushed on in the wake of the stampede, the posse siding him. Stragglers from the band of rustlers turned back, giving up the fight to contain the herd. They weren't in any mood to surrender, though. Gun flashes counterpointed the lightning strikes as isolated battles broke out between outlaws and posse members. Longarm shot two more men off their horses with the Winchester, then jammed the empty rifle back in the boot and drew his Colt.

He lifted his voice in a bellowing shout that beat futilely against the rolling thunder and the howling wind. "Rosa! Rosa, can you hear me?" For several minutes he continued calling her name, despair growing in him as he got no response.

But then, he thought he heard a snatch of a woman's scream, before the wind shredded the sound and carried it away. "Rosa!" he roared. "Rosa!"

"Custis! Help!"

By God, it *was* her! Longarm's pulse hammered inside his skull as he turned his horse and shouted her name again. He plunged toward where he thought her voice had been.

That was when the rain really hit.

Chapter 19

The rain struck him like a thousand, no, a million, tiny fists, battering him with such fury that he was nearly swept from the saddle. He clamped his knees against the buckskin and clung tightly to the reins. "Rosa!" he called again, but as he did so, he swallowed so much water that he almost choked.

He was blind now, as blind as if he had been at the bottom of a river. The sky was as dark as midnight. Only when lightning flashed could he see anything, and then only for a split second. But one of those fractions of a heartbeat illuminated a scene that etched itself on his brain. He saw Rosa stumbling toward him on foot, her long dark hair soaked and plastered to her head by the rain, her clothes clinging to her slender body.

He shouted her name again and slid from the saddle, being careful not to let go of the reins. If the buckskin got away, they would be lost out here in this chaos. He reached out toward the place where he had seen her, hoping to run into her in the darkness. Lightning flashed again.

Longarm's hand shot out during that instant he could see. His fingers closed around Rosa's arm and pulled her toward him. She grabbed him, crying and shaking and shuddering. The rain streamed down over and around them as he held her tightly, saying, "It's all right, it's all right. It's over now, Rosa."

But it wasn't. From the corner of his eye, during one of those brilliant flashes, he caught a glimpse of Arch Kellman riding toward them. The gun in Kellman's hand flared and bucked, but the sharp bark of its report was lost in the rolling thunder.

Longarm flung himself to the ground, diving to the side and hanging on to Rosa to take her with him. They hit and rolled, and the slashing hooves of Kellman's mount barely missed them. The sand had turned to a sea of mud. Longarm tried to keep his Colt out of it as he rolled over and came up on a knee. His other hand was on Rosa's shoulder, pressing her down. His finger was taut on the Colt's trigger . . .

But there was nothing to shoot at. He couldn't see anything.

If he couldn't see Kellman, Kellman couldn't see them, Longarm reasoned. He pushed himself to his feet and dragged Rosa up with him. Moving, he thought. They had to get moving. He had lost the buckskin's reins. The horse could be anywhere. So could Kellman. But standing still would increase the chances of the outlaw finding them.

Or was it the other way around? Longarm cudgeled his brain, trying to make it work properly in this madhouse of wind and rain and thunder and lightning.

Another flash. Kellman was only a few yards away, his back to them. Longarm snapped a shot at him. There were times when it was perfectly all right to shoot somebody in the back, and damned if this wasn't one of them, he thought. As darkness closed in again, though, he was convinced that he had missed. A second later he knew it because Kellman's gun roared. Longarm felt as much as heard the disturbance in the air as the bullet passed close by his ear.

He had heard the gun go off, he realized. Was the storm letting up, lessening in its ferocity? He thought maybe it was. But it still had plenty of punch, and a new gust of wind almost knocked him off his feet.

Something hit him, sent him spinning. He still had hold of Rosa's hand. She fell with him and screamed as she landed on top of him. He thought it had been Kellman's horse that clipped him, just as the Bloody Spaniard's mount had in the encounter a couple of nights earlier. He had nearly been trampled several times lately, and he was getting tired of it. He had to get Rosa off of him, had to get up before Kellman found them again.

Lightning tore through the sky, the brilliance of the flash making Longarm wince as it struck his eyes. But he could still see clearly enough to make out Kellman looming over them on horseback, aiming the pistol in his hand straight at the back of Rosa's head. Longarm had less than a split second in which to act. Moving as fast as he ever had in his life, he tipped up the barrel of his Colt and shoved his right hand under Rosa's left arm, between her arm and her body. His gun roared and so did Kellman's, the two shots coming so close together they sounded like one.

But Longarm's shot had come first, and Kellman's bullet sailed off harmlessly into the storm as the slug from Longarm's Colt ripped into his neck, just behind his jutting chin, and bored on up through his brain. The impact flipped him backward out of the saddle and off the horse. He hit the ground with a soggy thud.

Longarm heard that thud and knew now the storm was letting up. He held Rosa against him and rolled onto his side, keeping his gun pointed in the direction where Kellman had fallen. Kellman's horse bolted, racing off and disappearing into the downpour. Longarm realized he could see a little now, even when the lightning didn't flash. Conditions were definitely improving.

That was the way it was with these West Texas storms. They came fast, and they went fast.

Rosa shuddered and sobbed, but after a few minutes Longarm was able to convince her that Kellman was dead and she was safe. She clutched at him and said, "I . . . I was so scared, Custis! He said he would never let me go until he was tired of me, and then he would kill me! But then the storm came and I was able to break away from him . . . I ran and ran . . . I didn't know where I was going, I just wanted to be away from him . . . Then you were there." She lifted her head at last and looked at him, drops of rain rolling down her face like tears. Maybe they *were* tears. "The *Señor Dios* brought you to me, Custis. His hand guided you."

Longarm couldn't argue with that. In the midst of this hellish storm, it had taken more than luck to enable him to find her in time to save her from Kellman.

They rested a few minutes, and then Longarm got to his feet. He helped her up. She asked miserably, "What will we do now?"

"This storm may be passing on soon. When it does, we'll see if we can find a couple of horses. There ought to be several running around loose out here."

She caught at his arm. "Ramon?" she asked. "What do you know of him, and old Alejandro?"

"Alejandro made it into Tascosa looking for help after Kellman and his bunch hit your place. He was wounded but ought to be just fine."

"And Ramon?"

Longarm shrugged. "He was alive when we left him at the ranch. One of the men who knows something about doctoring stayed there to tend to him and then take him into town. He was shot up pretty bad, but he might have a chance. I just don't know."

Rosa rested her head against his shoulder for a few moments and cried a little more. He didn't begrudge her the release, not after everything she had been through. While she was sobbing, the rain slackened even more. It still fell steadily, but not that hard. And the wind had died down, too, along with the thunder and lightning.

Shoot, thought Longarm, it might not be long before the sun was out again.

"I am glad you killed him," said Rosa as they trudged along through the mud a while later. "I know that it is a sin to think such a thing, but I am glad anyway."

Longarm knew she was talking about Arch Kellman. "I don't exactly figure I'll lose much sleep over ventilating him," he said with a tired grin. His hat was lost, his clothes were soaked, the mud pulled at his boots with every step he took, and if there was a muscle in his body that didn't ache, he couldn't figure out which one it was. And despite all that, he felt just fine.

Of course, things hadn't worked out perfectly, not by a long shot. That herd of stolen cattle was scattered hell-west and crosswise, and it would take days, maybe even weeks, for them to all be rounded up again. But he intended to press the crews from the XIT and the other big ranches in the area into service to handle that roundup. He thought it was the least they could do since the gang of rustlers wouldn't be plaguing the Panhandle anymore.

Some of the outlaws might have survived, of course, although between the stampede, the storm, and the bullets of the posse, Longarm would have been willing to bet that most of them had gone under. The ones who hadn't been killed probably wouldn't ever show their faces in this part of the country again. Some of the posse members might have met their Maker, too, and Longarm regretted that. The survivors were probably just as scattered as those cattle. They would come dragging back to Tascosa on their own, though, and wouldn't have to be rounded up.

It was starting to look as if he and Rosa might have to

walk all the way to town. They hadn't come across any strays. If that was what it took, Longarm supposed that was what they would have to do. He had to get back to Tascosa one way or another, because there was one final bit of business he had to wrap up, one more lobo whose pelt he was after.

Or in this case, he thought, a suit of armor rather than a pelt.

The sun had come out, just like he'd thought it would, spreading its golden rays over a drenched landscape. Every little gully ran gurgling full of dirty brown water. That condition would last for several hours, maybe even overnight, but then the thirsty sands deep below the surface would suck down all the moisture and things would get back to normal.

Without the sunlight, he wouldn't have had any warning at all. As it was, he saw the sudden flash as the rays reflected off of something to his left. He started to swing in that direction, reaching for his Colt as he did so, but then something smashed into his arm and knocked him to the ground. Rosa screamed.

Longarm grunted in pain. His left arm was mostly numb and what wasn't numb hurt like blazes. Blood trickled onto the drying ground, more moisture for the sand to lap up. He didn't know how badly he was hurt, but he could still use his right arm. Again he reached for his Colt.

Another shot blasted, kicking up dirt from the ground near him. He froze, knowing the next shot might be fatal if he kept trying for the revolver. Rosa fell to her knees beside him, crying, "Custis! *Dios mio,* Custis!"

Funny thing about sunlight, he thought. It could conceal as well as reveal. Right now, it seemed to ripple in front of his eyes, blurring his vision. Or maybe that was just him. He could make out shapes, but that was all. Shapes coming toward him, and something that shone in the sun . . .

"The ghost," breathed Rosa. "*Ai*, the ghost of a conquistador . . ."

Longarm's vision cleared. He saw the Spaniard, the Bloody Spaniard, riding toward him, leading a heavily loaded packhorse. The armored figure wasn't carrying a saber or a lance, but a modern Winchester instead, the rifle he had used to shoot Longarm. What kind of conquistador carried a repeating rifle? thought Longarm.

Of course, the Spaniard wasn't a real conquistador. Hell, he wasn't even a Spaniard. He was bloody, though, no doubt about that. His hands were stained a deep, rich crimson from all the blood that had been spilled during the campaign of lawlessness he had orchestrated.

And now, from all appearances, he was running out, getting while the getting was good. Longarm had no doubt that the bulging *aparejos* on the packhorse were stuffed full of ill-gotten loot from the various jobs the gang had pulled under this man's direction.

The Spaniard brought his mount to a stop about ten feet away from Longarm and Rosa. Now that he was this close, Longarm could see that he had a black bandanna wrapped around the bottom half of his face under the plumed helmet. The armor didn't glow in broad daylight, either. Darkness was required for that. Now it had a dull shine to it, marred by the nicks and dents of centuries.

"Where'd you get the tin suit, Sheriff?" asked Longarm hoarsely. "Did you steal it from Professor Chapman?"

"So you figured out who I am." The high-pitched voice came from under the bandanna. With his free hand, the Spaniard reached up and took off the helmet, dropped it on the ground next to his horse. He pulled the bandanna down, revealing the florid face of Sheriff Clyde Thurston. "Hell, I don't reckon it matters. I was gonna kill you anyway. Before I do, though, I want to know who *you* are, Parker. You sure as hell ain't no grub line rider like you made out to be."

"Custis Long, deputy U.S. marshal out of Denver," grated Longarm.

Thurston nodded. "Yeah, I thought it must be somethin' like that. That other fella who come around askin' a bunch of questions a while back was a lawman, too. Private, though. A range detective, worked for the Cattleman's Association. They brung him in when all the rustlin' started. Didn't find that out until after I'd killed him, though."

"Because you went around killing anybody you thought might be a threat, without even finding out for sure if they knew who the Spaniard was. Like those two drunks, and Pete Brandywine, and your old friend Hobart Rhone. Even your own deputy!" Longarm couldn't keep the anger out of his voice.

"Fletch was too damn dedicated to the job for his own good. I kept tellin' him to be more like me, but he just wouldn't listen. Neither would Bart. Just kept on a-houndin' me, tellin' me I had to investigate and find out who was behind the outlaws. He didn't really know nothin'. I just got damned tired o' listenin' to him carry on like that." Thurston snorted. "Just because he said I ought to run for sheriff, that didn't give him no right to try to boss me around."

A harsh, humorless laugh came from Longarm. "It was sure as hell simple, when you come right down to it. Greed and laziness, that's all. You were smart enough to think of using that armor to make everybody scared of you, but in the end you just wanted a pile of loot."

"Well, sure. Ain't that what everybody wants?"

Longarm didn't waste any breath answering the question. His arm hurt too much for that.

"I really am curious, though," Thurston went on. "How'd you figure out it was me?"

"You overplayed your hand," said Longarm, forcing himself to ignore the pain. This was one instance in which stalling for time might not be a good thing, he thought.

If he passed out, Thurston could kill him and Rosa with no trouble. But right now, he didn't seem to have any choice but to keep talking. "That ambush started me thinking about you. After it was over, you almost killed me with that shotgun, and it would have looked like an accident. But I got to thinking about how well that would have worked out for you if you were the one who wanted me dead. After I saw you behind the Deuces and all the shooting started, you had time to shuck out of the armor and get around the building to the street, so you could finish me off, accidental-like, if your gunnies didn't do the job." Longarm took a deep breath. "After I thought of that, I remembered hearing somebody in the upstairs hall earlier in the afternoon, somebody whose walk had an odd sound to it. I realized the sound was because of that limp of yours. You were up there talking to Arabella."

"If you're worried that she was in on it with me, you can set your mind at ease, Long," said Thurston. "For what little time you got left, that is. Yeah, I was up there, but she didn't tip me off that you'd be comin' up those back stairs sometime after dark. Fact is, she wouldn't hardly give me the time o' day. I think I heard her mutter somethin' about me bein' a stupid lout, or somethin' like that. Guess I proved her wrong, though. Most folks think I don't pay much attention to what's goin' on around me, but the truth is, I watch real close all the time. I knew there was somethin' goin' on betwixt the two o' you, and when I saw one of the bartenders get one o' them fancy bottles of brandy out of the back room and put it where he could get to it easy, I figured he'd be takin' up to the Englishwoman's room later, for the supper you had planned." Thurston sneered. "So you're just a lucky guesser, Long, nothin' more."

Slowly, Longarm shook his head. "Nope. I had proof."

"Proof?" The dogleg sheriff snorted in disbelief. "What proof?"

"Right out of your own mouth, this morning when you said something about me being shot at on the back stairs last night." Longarm grinned. "I didn't mention that after the shooting. All I said was that somebody bushwhacked me while I was in the back alley. For you to know I was actually on the stairs, you had to be there."

Thurston glared at him, opened and closed his mouth a couple of times, finally said, "Damn! Well, it ain't gonna do you no good. Time to die now." He lifted the barrel of the Winchester a little. "You ready?"

Rosa whimpered and huddled closer against Longarm's side. He winced as she jostled his wounded arm, but he didn't say anything to her. Instead, he forced the grin back onto his face and said, "The only other thing I want to know is how a big ol' tub of lard like you even fits into that armor, Thurston."

With his face twisting in hate, Thurston brought the rifle up even more, ready to fire. Longarm's Colt blasted first, the gun that he had felt Rosa slip out of the holster a moment earlier as she pretended to cower in fear against him. Now the gun bucked again, steady in her hand. Both bullets smashed into the armored torso of the man on the horse, rocking him back in the saddle. Thurston dropped both the reins and the Winchester. Spooked by the shooting and the smell of powder smoke and blood, the horse bolted.

Longarm forced himself onto his feet. Rosa came up with him and pressed the butt of the Colt into his hand. He lifted the pistol and squeezed off two more shots after the figure on the racing horse. Thurston toppled out of the saddle, smashing heavily to the ground.

He rolled over and got up, though, and started to stagger away. Longarm started after him, but Rosa clutched his arm. "Let him go!" she begged. "We are safe now, and he is wounded. He cannot go far."

"Can't risk it," muttered Longarm. "I got to see it

through. He caused too much suffering, too much death, to let him get away now." He shook off her hand and went after the shambling figure in armor.

Longarm wasn't in much better shape than Thurston, though, and he knew it. He had lost enough blood from the wound in his arm so that his head was spinning. Stubbornly, he forced himself on. Just as stubbornly, Rosa came with him, carrying the Winchester Thurston had dropped.

Longarm heard a roaring sound and saw that Thurston had stopped up ahead, about fifty yards away. As Longarm came closer, he saw that Thurston stood on the edge of a gully, one of the normally dry arroyos that was now full of runoff from the earlier storm. There was no way to cross it, no way of knowing how deep the water was.

"Give it up, Thurston!" Longarm called to him. "It's over!"

Thurston turned, producing a pistol from somewhere under the armor. Longarm and Rosa were both ready to fire, but before Thurston could get off a shot, he stumbled backward. That armor was heavy, and a small section of the bank at the edge of the arroyo had given way. With a startled scream, Thurston fell back into the muddy, fast-flowing water.

Longarm and Rosa hurried forward. As they approached the arroyo, they saw Thurston's head surface once, for an instant, but then the swift current and the weight of the conquistador's armor pulled him back down. He didn't come up again.

They were still standing there a moment later when they heard a loud hail.

Longarm turned his head to see what was coming now, hoping that it wasn't more trouble. In his long career as a lawman, he had seldom been more beaten up and tuckered out than he was right now. To his relief, he saw a couple of men riding toward them, leading some riderless horses. He recognized them as two members of the posse.

Longarm cast one more glance at the raging river in the arroyo where Thurston had disappeared. "Damn it," he muttered. "He never did tell me where he got that suit of armor, or how he got it to glow."

Rosa laughed wearily and leaned her head against his shoulder. "Must you know everything?"

"Well," groused Longarm, "it'd be nice."

Then he up and passed out.

Thurston hadn't stolen the armor from Professor Chapman, and the professor was mighty upset when he heard about Thurston washing away in the flood while he was wearing it.

"My God, what a find! I'm going with them when they go out to search for the sheriff's body. Perhaps the armor can still be recovered."

Longarm figured that was pretty likely. Once the water went down, it wouldn't be much of a chore to find Thurston's body.

That was exactly the way it happened. Longarm was at the doctor's house a few days later, his arm in a sling, visiting with Rosa and Ramon and Alejandro, when a group of searchers came in with Thurston's corpse draped over a saddle. Chapman was with them, carrying the armor in his wagon.

Ramon was still pale, but he was on his way to recovery from the bullet wounds he had suffered in Kellman's raid on the Hernandez ranch. It would be a while before he was on his feet again. In the meantime, Rosa and Alejandro would take care of the place, with some help from some XIT cowboys. The XIT planned to buy the Box B from Barfield's heir, a female cousin who lived back in St. Louis. Longarm figured the syndicate had their eye on the Hernandez place, too, but they might have a hard time prying it away. Rosa and Ramon still intended to make a go of it. And Longarm wasn't going to bet against them.

"So you admit, Ramon, that not all gringos are evil?" Rosa prodded her brother. "Señor Long, for example . . . ?"

Grudgingly, Ramon said, "We owe Señor Long a great debt. Honor demands that we pay it by calling him our friend."

"And welcoming him on the Eagle Ranch whenever he wishes to visit?" said Rosa.

Ramon summoned up a smile and nodded. "Of course."

Longarm returned the smile and said, "I appreciate that, Ramon. Expect it'll be a while before I get down this way again, though. If I know my boss, soon as I get back to Denver he'll have a whole heap of work for me to do."

"A man cannot work all the time," said Alejandro. The old-timer had bounced back from his injury with surprising resilience. "There must be wine, and good food, and singing, and pretty señoritas."

Longarm laughed. "I can't argue with that, old son."

A little while later, after leaving the doctor's house, he and Rosa strolled on the boardwalk along Tascosa's main street. Her left arm was linked with his right. Up ahead was the Deuces.

"Why is it, Custis," asked Rosa, "that you never told me about this intimate dinner you had planned with Lady Arabella Winthrop?"

Longarm frowned. "What was it you asked me a few days ago, out there by that arroyo? Must you know everything?"

She laughed, but there was an edge to it. Longarm looked at the Deuces and thought he saw Arabella peering out over the batwings at the entrance.

Lord, Lord, he thought. Suddenly the idea of going back to Denver and having Billy Vail send him out to get shot at again didn't sound half bad.

Watch for

LONGARM AND THE GRAND
CANYON GANG

303rd novel in the exciting LONGARM series
from Jove

Coming in February!